D0830954

**'He'll be okay.'**

Sara wanted to touch him, but didn't dare. After what they'd done this evening no touch from her could be construed as pure consolation. And what they'd both wanted to do was hovering between them now, like a wayward genie that had popped out of a bottle and refused to be crammed back into confinement again.

'Yeah. I hope so. That was a good spot there, Sara.' He said the words awkwardly, as if even that might be construed as being inappropriate.

'Thanks. For listening to what I said.'

'Why shouldn't I?'

She shrugged. 'Oh, you know. Doctors don't always listen to paramedics.'

'A good doctor listens to everyone.'

'Yeah. Good doctors do that.'

He grinned, dipping his head slightly in a gesture of acknowledgement. In the last two hours they'd gone from housemates to almost-lovers, and now they were colleagues. And colleagues seemed to be thc only one of the three options where they could breathe, where they both knew what to do and how to act. Maybe from here they could work their way through to being friends, so that when the time came for them to part they could do it well.

It sounded like a plan, anyway. It was the only one Sara had, so it had better work…

**Dear Reader**

One of the best things about being a writer is that you have the opportunity to travel, even if it's only in your imagination. So this book has been a real indulgence, because I got to set it in two of my favourite places—which just happen to be on opposite sides of the world.

For me, one of the best parts of travelling is returning home. But for Sara and Reece 'home' isn't just a different place on the map, it's an entirely different concept. The challenge that they face is not merely a matter of physical distance, and it's one which is far more difficult to overcome. I loved writing their story, even if they did have me tearing my hair out at times, and I was with them every step of the way on their travels as they explored each other's worlds and began to find that home truly is where the heart is.

Thank you for reading Reece and Sara's story. I hope you enjoy it. I'm always delighted to hear from readers, and you can email me via my website at: www.annieclaydon.com

*Annie*

# THE REBEL AND MISS JONES

BY
ANNIE CLAYDON

All the characters in this book have no existence outside the imagination of the author, and have no relation whatsoever to anyone bearing the same name or names. They are not even distantly inspired by any individual known or unknown to the author, and all the incidents are pure invention.



First published in Great Britain 2013
by Mills & Boon, an imprint of Harlequin (UK) Limited.
Harlequin (UK) Limited, Eton House, 18-24 Paradise Road,
Richmond, Surrey TW9 1SR



ISBN: 978 0 263 23349 0



Harlequin (UK) policy is to use papers that are natural, renewable and recyclable products and made from wood grown in sustainable forests. The logging and manufacturing process conform to the legal environmental regulations of the country of origin.

Printed and bound in Great Britain
by CPI Antony Rowe, Chippenham, Wiltshire

Cursed from an early age with a poor sense of direction and a propensity to read, **Annie Claydon** spent much of her childhood lost in books. After completing her degree in English Literature, she indulged her love of romantic fiction and spent a long, hot summer writing a book of her own. It was duly rejected and life took over. A series of U-turns led in the unlikely direction of a career in computing and information technology, but the lure of the printed page proved too much to bear, and she now has the perfect outlet for the stories which have always run through her head, writing Medical Romance™ for Mills and Boon®. Living in London, a city where getting lost can be a joy, she has no regrets for having taken her time in working her way back to the place that she started from.

**Recent titles by Annie Claydon:**

THE DOCTOR MEETS HER MATCH
DOCTOR ON HER DOORSTEP
ALL SHE WANTS FOR CHRISTMAS

To the unsung hero

## CHAPTER ONE

'I'VE got to go. You know that, don't you?'

They'd been through this already. Sara grinned up at her brother. 'Of course I do. I know what it's like to be on call. You can't tell a bush fire that now's not convenient and you'll be there in a couple of days.'

Simon smiled for the first time since he'd answered the telephone that morning. 'You grew up some time when I wasn't looking. I keep forgetting that.' He pinched the bridge of his nose, as if he still couldn't believe the evidence of his own eyes. 'Ten years is a long time.'

And a lot had happened in the years since they'd last seen each other. But this wasn't the time to dwell on that. 'If the boot was on the other foot, and that phone call had been for a paramedic, you wouldn't have seen me for dust. You need to go.'

Simon shrugged. 'You'll be here when I get back?' It was almost as if he thought she wouldn't. As if the bonds that they'd been carefully rebuilding for the last two days would break at the slightest touch. Sara could understand that too. She shared his fears.

'Where else am I going to go? By the time you get back I'll have got over my jet-lag, rearranged your house for you and taught Trader how to bark with an English accent.'

'I've still got an English accent.' Simon frowned. 'Haven't I?'

'Now you mention it, no. Not any more.' Simon's accent was pure Aussie to her ears. He'd changed in other ways too. No longer the lanky older brother, fresh out of university, who had clashed so violently with their mother and walked out of their lives for ever. He was broader, more thoughtful and a great deal more measured. Much tidier too. 'Did I say that I'm proud of you?'

'No. But thanks.' The smile he gave her was full of the warmth they'd once had. Simon heaved his backpack onto his shoulder and turned to face her squarely. 'I'll let someone know you're here as soon as I get to the CFA centre. There's a list of numbers on the pad in the kitchen, so call if you need anything. Someone will come by tomorrow if I'm not back.'

'I'll be okay. I'm not sixteen any more.'

'Bear with me. The fire's well out of this region and heading westwards, away from us, but if there is any danger someone will contact you and drive up here to get you. If you can put your valuables into one bag, well and good, but don't waste any time...'

'I know, I know.' Sara held up her hands. 'We've been through all this.'

'Right.' Simon still hesitated. Finally he leant in, giving her an awkward kiss on the cheek.

'Stay safe. See you soon.' Sara gave him a bright smile, and propelled him out of the door.

She'd been restless all day, and had hovered fitfully between being half asleep and half awake all night, but now something shocked Sara into wakefulness. The silence perhaps. Or maybe it was the insidious, nagging worry that she had tried think through logically but still couldn't quite put a name to. Even the feeble light of early dawn somehow seemed slightly menacing.

Simon might have come back while she was sleeping. The thought propelled her out of bed, and took her all the way to the large windows at the front of the house. Nothing. His car wasn't parked in its usual place, and his jacket wasn't hanging in the hallway. Sara knew that she wouldn't find him sleeping in his bedroom either, but she looked anyway.

She wasn't used to this. She'd dealt with her fair share of emergencies but waiting it out while someone else handled the situation was way out of her experience. Taking Trader for a long, brisk walk yesterday afternoon, without seeing another living soul, had spooked her even more. She'd returned to Simon's beautiful house, switched on the TV and played one DVD after another, just to hear the sound of human voices.

She padded to the kitchen, the sound of scratching at the back door coming almost as a relief. Pulling back the bolts, she opened the door, and fifty pounds of Australian cattle dog, the only one of his kind that Sara had ever seen before, herded her deftly out of the way to get past her and into the house.

'Whoa, Trader.' The dog had followed her footsteps, trotting hopefully to Simon's bedroom door, and finding the room empty, was now pacing the hallway fretfully. 'He's not here. I'm on breakfast duty today.'

Trader was unsettled about something. Perhaps food would appease him. Fetching the plastic container that held his food, Sara made for the doors that led out onto the veranda, unlocking them and sliding them back.

Maybe the wind changed. Maybe it was just that she was outside the house now. The smell hit her like a slap in the face. Blown in on the breeze, like bad news from across the hillside, came the acrid smell of smoke.

Trader was at her side, pressing himself against her legs, and she staggered back. He nipped at her heels, trying to shepherd her back into the house, and Sara grabbed his collar. 'Okay, okay, have it your way.' Maybe Trader knew best. She certainly didn't know what to do.

Gathering up his bowls, spilling what was left of the water in one down her nightdress, she pulled the dog inside the house and shut the patio doors, locking them tight as if somehow that might stop a fire from getting in. 'You can eat inside today.'

Quickly she put Trader's food down for him on the kitchen floor and made for the sink to fill his water bowl. When she twisted the tap, nothing happened. Sara whirled around and saw that the LED lights on the fridge and the cooker were out too.

'Dammit!' No electricity meant that the pump from the water tank wasn't working. Turning the tap off, she poured some spring water from the refrigerator into Trader's bowl, then took a swig from the bottle. Maybe the hydration would help her to think.

This must be another fire. Unless the wind had changed and the fire that Simon had gone to was coming this way. Sara had no idea, and it didn't really matter. It looked as if the situation had changed, and so Simon needed to keep his promise and either come and get her himself or send someone. Any time now would be good.

The phone was dead and even though she knew her mobile was out of range here, she tried it anyway. 'It's only a little smoke, Trader. Smoke travels for miles, the fire's probably nowhere near us.'

Her assertion was born of hope rather than knowledge, but at least Trader's gentle, intelligent eyes looked convinced. Perhaps that was a good sign. Sara left him to eat, and ran to fetch the binoculars that Simon kept in his home office. Slipping outside, she trained them on the horizon in the direction that the smoke seemed to be coming from.

She could see the source of the black smoke, which billowed out from behind a fold in the landscape. It was impossible to gauge how close the fire was or which way it was headed, but the breeze in her face gave Sara a sickening clue.

'Oh!' Her chest and stomach tightened painfully, and she doubled over, trying to breathe. She had to get out of here. Had to get home. She had responsibilities.

Suddenly this whole trip seemed impossibly reckless. Gran had urged her to come here, and had even booked herself into respite care for three weeks, but that was just temporary. She was ninety years old, and completely dependent on Sara. What would she do if she didn't come back?

Simon would send someone. He had to. Their mother might have labelled her elder brother feckless, irresponsible and not worthy of a moment in their thoughts, but Sara knew that wasn't true. This time he was going to come through for her.

Self-pity wasn't going to get her anywhere. Emptying the contents of the kitchen drawers at least secured a battery radio and Sara switched it on, scanning for a local station. Surely they'd be putting out information on some kind of regular basis.

Carrying the radio with her, she quickly filled a couple of bags with what she hoped were Simon's most valued possessions and put them in the hall. She pulled on a pair of jeans and made her way around the outside of the house, pulling the fire shutters down over the windows and back door as Trader ran back and forth, trying to urge her away from the ever more pungent smell of smoke, which was beginning to hang in the air like a dirty fog.

A tone sounded from the radio, and she held it to her ear, straining to catch every word. It didn't help much, mentioning places that she'd only half heard of and could be anywhere, and fire alert statuses that could mean anything. She understood the urgency, though. *Evacuate. Be safe. Nearest low-risk area.*

There was nowhere to go. She was without a car and even if she could remember the way to the nearest town, she knew that trying to walk the twenty or so miles there would be madness. Simon had designed this house himself, and put all his architectural expertise and experience of local building techniques and conditions into it. The shutters were designed to keep burning embers from getting into the house, and the mud-brick walls would afford some protection if the blaze was not too intense. If the worst came to the worst, she and Trader were just going to have to sit it out and hope for the best.

The thought made her feel sick. Gulping back tears, Sara turned to the only living creature that might give her any comfort. 'He won't forget us, Trader.' The animal seemed to sense her anxiety and nosed at her hand. 'It's probably not as bad as we think it is. Perhaps the wind will change…'

She stiffened, straining to see, as she caught a glimpse of something that looked like more smoke, this time on the dirt road leading to the front of the house. There was movement, and the flash of something bright in the sunlight. Just as dread began to grip her, squeezing all of the air from her lungs, she made out what it was. A vehicle, moving at speed and kicking up dust as it went. It could only be coming to one place. That track only led here.

Not wanting to leave anything to chance, Sara ran back into the house, pulling the red tablecloth from the table and sending the wooden bowls in the centre of it crashing to the floor behind her. Whoever it was wouldn't be able to hear her yet, but she shouted anyway, waving the table-cloth over her head.

'Sit, Trader.' Sara strained to see any sign that the driver of the SUV had seen her. Nothing. She waved the cloth again and this time, through her tears of frustration, she saw something. Headlights, three short flashes and then a pause, and another three flashes. Just to make sure, she waved again. Another three flashes.

'Thank you.' She whispered the words under her breath, to no one in particular, her chest heaving. 'It's all right, see, Trader. Someone's coming.'

By the time the SUV had skidded to a halt outside the house Trader was barking joyfully, pulling her towards the man who swung the door open and got out.

She could have hugged him. If he'd been middle-aged, with a paunch, she might have. But this was the kind of man you didn't just walk up to and hug without having to accuse yourself of an ulterior motive. Tall, broad and with blue eyes, bright against his tanned skin. Thick blond hair that looked as if it hadn't been combed in a while, which just added to the general look of a handsome adventurer.

'Sara? Sara Jones?' He was striding towards her and she nodded, lost for words. 'Simon sent me to fetch you.'

This wasn't the moment to ask why he hadn't come sooner. Neither was it the time for the normal reservations about getting into strangers' cars. Trader seemed to know him and at his command gave off trying to lick his hand and trotted to the SUV, jumping in and settling quietly on the back seat.

'We have to hurry.' The stranger didn't seem disposed to stop for questions anyway, and had already taken the steps up to the veranda two at a time, twisting the handle of the front door and turning to her in surprise when it didn't budge.

'I've got the key here.' Sara hurried after him, pulling the single key from her pocket. In her agitation it slipped through her fingers, bouncing next to her bare feet on the decking and sliding through a crack between the boards.

At least he didn't call her stupid, but that didn't stop Sara from muttering the word under her breath. He shrugged, starting for the back of the house, and Sara ran after him. 'I locked the doors at the back too. Maybe we could lever one of the boards up. I think I can get my arm through...'

He looked at her in frank disbelief. 'Yeah, maybe. Stand back.' Before she could stop him he had shouldered the door and it burst inwards, snapping back against the wall.

'Did you have to do that?' The door had smashed into the table in the hallway, sending a glass bowl crashing onto the floor, and broken shards were everywhere. Just because her habit of locking doors was a little over the top for this neck of the woods, it didn't mean he had to go caveman on her.

He turned, taking her by the shoulders. 'Sara, we don't have any time.' The look on his face was making her tremble.

'But you can't even see the fire yet...'

'If you can see a fire, it's too late to run. At the moment we have two options, staying here to fight it or getting out. We're not properly prepared for the first and the second isn't going to be available for much longer.' He was focussed, calm, and Sara began to divine that breaking the door down had not been an overreaction. 'It's going to be okay, Sara, but if we're leaving, we need to do it now.'

There was something in his eyes that made her trust him. Something about the brief smile he gave her. She'd made a few bad decisions in her life, but hopefully this wasn't going to be one of them. 'Yes...okay.'

'Good. Thank you.' Before she could ask him what would happen next, he had lifted her up in his arms, carrying her into the house, his boots scrunching on the broken glass. 'Have you got a pair of heavy boots and a thick cotton jacket?'

'Yes. But it's too hot...'

'Heavy clothes will protect you. Cotton is less flammable than man-made materials.' There was no arguing with him, and Sara didn't particularly want him to elaborate on a situation where she might need heavy cotton clothing to protect her. Hopefully he was just being over-cautious.

He let her down, and she bolted to her bedroom. Now wasn't the time to be thinking that despite the smoky smell of his clothes the scent of his skin was alluring, or that the sheer power in his arms and shoulders was somehow reassuring.

When she emerged from her room, the hallway was empty of the bundles that she'd left there and her new companion was rummaging in the refrigerator, two large bottles of water under his arm.

'Ready to go?'

'Yes.' She mustn't hesitate now. Mustn't go and check the house to make sure everything was secure. If Simon had trusted this stranger, then she had to do so.

'Good.' He turned to her, kicking the fridge door closed. His gaze flicked over her with an audacity that made her shiver, and Sara called a mental reality check. He was just making sure that she wasn't wearing anything that might catch light. 'Have you got everything?'

'Yes.' Her passport and valuables were in the large leather handbag she had slung across her body. That was all she needed.

'Let's go, then.'

He hurried her to the SUV and then went back to draw the shutter down over the shattered front door. Sara craned her neck to keep the house in view as the car described a wide arc and bumped back down the dirt track towards the road.

'Reece Fletcher. Nice to meet you, Sara.'

'What?' All her attention was on the house, trying to fix it into her memory as if that would somehow ensure that it would still be standing when she returned. It had been Simon's dream to build this house, and the thought of it being reduced to ashes was impossibly cruel.

'Will you keep your eye on the road ahead of us for me?'

'What for?' She swung round, scanning the empty road, before she realised that Reece was just giving her something to do so she wouldn't be staring out of the back window of the car for the next five miles, straining for a last glimpse of the house.

'Just look.' His voice was gentler now. 'And if you could open one of those bottles of water, that would be great. You'll find a couple of plastic beakers in the glove compartment.'

'Right.' Now that they were on the road, the lines of tension in Reece's face had relaxed and Sara drew her sunglasses out of her bag and put them on, only partly to shade her eyes from the glare. At least when he'd been ordering her around, she'd been able to respond without feeling the need to cry on his shoulder.

Time for another reality check. She'd just been rescued. Wanting to cling to Reece was a perfectly natural reaction. Deal with it.

'Nice to meet you too, Reece. Thanks for coming.' She handed him half a cup of water and he downed it in one go, passing the cup back to her for a refill.

'No worries. I'll phone Simon when we get into range of a signal, let him know that we're on our way.' Although the road was empty, he was still watchful, his gaze flipping constantly from the road to the rear-view mirrors.

'Thanks.' Sara supposed that she ought to ask, even if she didn't much want to know why it had taken so long for Reece to come for her. 'Where is he?'

'He's okay, but he's in the hospital. No burns, but he has a compound break to his leg. That means—'

'I know.' Sara struggled to control the panic which rose in her chest. 'I mean, I know what that means, I'm a paramedic.'

He nodded slowly, as if he'd just remembered. 'Then you'll know that he needed an operation to set the leg. That was done last night, and he's awake now and doing well. He has a crush fracture in his lower back, but that will mend with rest. Some smoke inhalation, but it wasn't too bad.'

'What happened to him?'

'I don't know the details. He was working on a firebreak when he was injured. They brought him out and airlifted him to hospital. I'm on his list of people to call in case of an accident.'

It was obvious that Simon should choose someone who lived more locally than she did for that, but it still hurt. 'And he didn't think to mention that I was out here with Trader?'

Reece shot her a questioning look, the edges of his mouth turned down. 'He was diverted on his way into the CFA centre, never got the opportunity to tell anyone. And after he was injured he was heavily sedated most of the time. I didn't know you were here and assumed that Trader was with a neighbour and that the house was empty. If it's anyone's fault, it's mine.'

The way he sprang to Simon's defence so readily warmed Sara. 'No one knew.' She puffed out a breath.

He turned in his seat slightly, shooting her a quizzical look. 'How long *have* you been here?'

'Three days. We wanted a week to ourselves so we could do some catching up. Next week was going to be for introductions to friends.'

Reece chuckled. 'If he'd mentioned that, I'd have known what I had to look forward to when I came up at the weekend.'

Light dawned. 'So you're the doctor he talks about? Fletch?'

He grinned at her and Sara's fingertips began to tingle. So he wasn't just a handsome face, he'd been a good friend to her brother. Simon hadn't mentioned that Fletch was gorgeous but, then, she supposed he wouldn't have noticed. She'd noticed, though.

'What's he been telling you?' The engine of the SUV raced up a gear. Simon hadn't said anything about that easy, intimate grin either.

'He says…that you're a doctor. And that you've worked in lots of different places, from city hospitals to the outback. It must be interesting.' That seemed safe enough. 'What does he say about me?'

'That you were just a kid when he left home.' There was a trace of seriousness in his voice. 'I've obviously got some catching up to do.'

He was deliberately not saying everything, but now wasn't the time to start wondering how much Reece knew about the dysfunctional branch of Simon's family. 'So how come you got to drive all the way out here? Surely this is a busy time for you, with the fires and everything.'

He laughed. 'I've been working for a week straight now. When the call came in about Simon, I was just about to go off duty and catch some shut-eye. By the time I got to the hospital, he'd just woken up and was shouting the place down and I came straight here.'

'So...' Her brain was working overtime, trying to process all of the new information that had been thrown at her this morning. She decided to concentrate on the most immediate concern. 'How long since you've slept?'

He laughed. 'Just keep talking.'

# CHAPTER TWO

SIMON's kid sister had taken it almost as a personal affront when he declined her offer to drive. Reece was tired but he wasn't that far gone. And ever since he'd seen Sara he'd been wide awake. Her dark hair, cut almost boyishly short, emphasised the soft curve at the nape of her neck. Those large, grey eyes managed to be both seductive and intelligent at the same time. She'd buckled down and done what had needed to be done in a crisis.

Clearly she was stubborn too. 'I'm perfectly capable of driving an automatic. I drive in London every day. Have you ever driven through a two-mile traffic jam to get to a pile-up?'

She had him there. 'Okay, but the conditions here are different.' He couldn't quite divine whether she had been aware of the seriousness of the situation. She was either handling it extremely well or she didn't realise how narrow their escape had been.

'All right, then. What do I need to watch out for?' She obviously wasn't about to give up, and exhilaration flared in the pit of Reece's stomach.

'Kangaroos on the road, for a start.' He reckoned she hadn't come across that one.

'Simon's told me about not trying to overtake them. I reckon I'm in much better shape than you are to keep an eye out for anything about to leap out in front of me, and I know where the brake is.' She wrinkled her nose at him, and Reece wondered how long he could hold out if she was going to use such unscrupulous methods of persuasion.

She had half turned towards him in her seat, and even though he couldn't see her eyes behind her sunglasses, he was pretty sure that she was sizing him up. 'So are you going to stop, or do we need to do that thing they do in the movies, where they keep driving while they swap places? I've not done that before, but I can give it a try.'

He found himself wondering whether she would actually do it, and a laugh began to rumble deep in his chest, leaving him almost breathless.

'What's that?' Her attention was diverted for a moment and the tone of her voice changed. Reece followed the line of her pointing finger and saw a ute stopped at the side of a track leading to the road.

Without a word, Reece swung the steering-wheel round, bumping onto the cracked, dry earth. She had the presence of mind to hang on, and they sped towards the vehicle. The hazards were on, blinking a warning, or in these circumstances more likely a cry for help.

'There's someone in there.' She was leaning forward, trying to see through the dust. Reece jammed on the brakes, and before he could tell her to stay in the car, she had released her seat belt and had jumped out, running towards the stranded truck.

He was right behind her. A quick look told him all he needed to know, and he opened the driver's door and spoke quietly to the middle-aged man behind the wheel.

'What's up, mate?' Blue lips. Perspiration. Gasping for breath. 'I'm a doctor.'

'Bloody angina. Always seems to come on just when

you don't want it, eh?' The man seemed more annoyed than relieved to scc them.

Reece resisted the temptation to roll his eyes. Bravado was just one of the unhelpful reactions that someone might have to a situation like this. 'Have you got medication? Pills or a spray?'

'Yes.' The man tried to turn in his seat and winced, clutching his chest. 'There's a spray in the emergency bag behind my seat.'

'I'll get it.' Sara was grinning, only a slight shake of her head betraying that she was probably thinking exactly the same as Reece was. Opening the passenger door, she clambered inside, tugging at the red canvas bag that was wedged behind the driver's seat. She managed to pull it out, almost falling backwards out of the vehicle, and unzipped it. 'Gotcha.'

'That's the one.' Disarmed by her smile, the man began to relax in his seat.

She passed the canister of nitroglycerin spray over to Reece, and he checked the prescription details on the label. 'Here you go, mate.'

The spray began to work, and almost before his eyes the man began to recover, the blue tinge around his lips fading. Reece straightened and beckoned Sara to his side, out of earshot. 'I'll check that the truck's running all right and then I want you to take my car. Keep going on this road for another thirty kilometres and we'll meet you…'

'I'll stay with you.' She grabbed the car keys from him and pocketed them. 'How long do we have?' She scanned the horizon, suddenly tense.

Reece didn't know. The fire might be coming this way and it might not. But by the time he got on the road again she could put at least five kilometres between herself and here and that could only be good. 'Not enough time to argue about it.'

'Perfect.' She turned on her heel and almost flounced the two steps back to the truck, bending down by the driver's door to talk to the man.

Reece sighed. The look on her face when she'd looked back in the direction they'd just come from told him that she had understood the risks of staying any longer, and her body language now showed that there was no changing her mind. And since he would have made the same decision in her place, he couldn't think of a single argument to persuade her differently.

'Right, then, Frank, if you're up to standing, we'll just move you round to the passenger seat and we can get going.' She gave the man a bright smile and he grinned at her. She had a way with her. No-nonsense, but with a lightness of touch that made even Reece feel better about the situation.

'Sure.' The man took her arm, leaning heavily on it, and Reece supported him from the other side. They slowly walked him around to the passenger seat and she folded a rug to make a support for his back, and buckled the seat belt over him.

'Where are we going?' That hint of tension had returned, although she hid it from Frank.

'It's thirty kilometres to the next town. I'll call ahead, see if an ambulance can meet us there.'

'Okay. I'll follow you.'

'Think you can keep up?' Reece grinned at her, suddenly relishing the chance to goad her a little.

Her cheeks flushed prettily and suddenly the day seemed a whole lot easier. 'I'll do my best.'

They leaned against the SUV side by side, drinking the takeaway coffee that Sara had got from the store in the main street while Reece had been busy seeing Frank into the ambulance. Trader lapped greedily at the water that she had poured into a camping dish she found in the boot of the car. 'So what was he doing out there? The guy in the café said that whole area is on high alert.'

'It is. He'd been staying with his daughter for a couple of days and he reckoned he'd nip back and get some things from home. He would have been fine if the angina hadn't slowed him up.'

'Hmm. So you gave him the talk about not being indestructible, then?'

Reece chuckled. He liked the way that she anticipated him. The way that they'd fallen into an almost seamless synchronicity back there. Just training, he guessed, hers and his. 'Yeah. I imagine he'll hear it again from a few different directions.'

She shrugged. 'Well, as long as he listens to one of them. We must be in mobile range by now.'

'Yeah. I'll call the hospital and get them to tell Simon that we're on our way. We can stop by at my house first and you can have a shower and change your clothes.' Reece drew his phone out of his pocket.

She twisted her mouth ruefully and Reece wondered what her lips would taste like. Sweet, he reckoned. Like the rest of her. 'I'll take the shower, but I don't have a change of clothes with me.'

'Wasn't that your case I put in the back of the car?' The large, lightweight case with a strip of gaudy material tied around the handle so it could be picked out easily at an airport.

'Yes, but my clothes are in the chest of drawers in Simon's spare room. I filled my case with his things.' She shrugged. 'It's his home. I wanted to bring as much of it as I could.'

Most women would have brought at least a change of clothes, but it seemed that Sara wasn't most women. She'd left behind practically everything she possessed in this hemisphere, putting her brother first. That simple act of selflessness made Reece smile.

'I'll call my sister, then. She's about your size. I dare say she can fix you up with something.'

She blushed again. Reece could really get used to that. 'That's okay. I have plenty of spending money. I can pop to the shops somewhere. I don't need much.'

Maybe not. But Reece could provide her with whatever she did need. She was his friend's sister, and she had no one else, which made her his responsibility now. 'I won't ask Kath to bring much, then.'

She nodded, head down all of a sudden, staring at her coffee. 'Thanks. Just a clean T-shirt would be great.' She drained her coffee, crushing the cardboard cup in her hands. 'Thanks for coming to get me. I don't know where I'd be right now if you hadn't.'

Her hands were shaking. She was under no illusions about the danger of the situation she'd been in.

'No problem. Do you want to drive while I make my calls? I'll programme the sat nav for you.' It might take her mind off the worries of the moment.

She nodded. 'Yeah. Thanks.'

'On the right, remember.' Reece tried to make a joke of it, but he was too tired to even see whether she got it or not.

'I remember. Get in, before I decide to leave you behind.'

He'd dozed fitfully in the car. As soon as he'd made his calls and there was nothing left to do, his body seemed to shut down, taking what it needed. Sara knew all about that kind of exhaustion. After her mother had died last year, finally losing her battle with cancer, it had been weeks before she'd been able to sit down without going to sleep. Gran had said she had slept off all her tears, gently making it clear that she disapproved of such a strategy, and in hindsight she might have been right.

The sat nav beeped in an indication that she was exactly where she was supposed to be. Sara nudged Reece gently, and he woke with a start, suddenly alert. 'Is this your house?'

'Uh?' He relaxed back into his seat when he saw where they were. 'No. This is my sister's house. Back up a bit, will you?'

Sara manoeuvred the heavy vehicle into the mouth of the driveway, stopping when Reece shook his head. 'Her car's not there, she must be over at my place. I'm just down the road a little way.'

'Down the road a little way' turned out to be more than four kilometres. Reece indicated an opening in the tall bushes that flanked the road, and Sara steered into it, the SUV dwarfing the small shiny runaround already parked outside the house.

'Here we are.' He grinned, stretching the kinks out of his back and shoulders. 'Hopefully, Kath's got the kettle on.' He opened the passenger door and almost fell out of the car, regaining his footing quickly. At his command, Trader suddenly woke from his repose and scrambled past Sara to follow Reece.

The house seemed far too big for one but, then, there was more space out here. There were large windows, a covered porch, and trees and bushes that were unfamiliar to Sara. It wasn't like home. From what Simon had said, it wasn't really a home to Reece either. Just a place to camp out until Reece's permanently itchy feet became too much for him and he upped sticks and moved on.

It was nice, though. An oasis of shade and weather-worn colours, which made up in charm for what it lacked in grooming. Reece fitted in here perfectly.

'Ah!' He was standing in the open doorway. 'I can smell fresh coffee.'

'Only because I brought it with me.' A woman's voice sounded from the hall. 'When did you last go shopping for food, Reece?'

He rolled his eyes and winked at Sara. 'I've been working.'

'Yeah, and what's your excuse the rest of the time?' A blonde, pretty woman dressed in shorts and a T-shirt joined him in the doorway.

Reece shrugged. 'No clue. Playing?'

Kath jabbed one finger at his ribs and Reece caught her hand, chuckling. Trader sensed that it was time to let off a little steam and threw himself against Reece's legs, demanding attention.

'Come inside.' Kath had broken away from Reece and was advancing on Sara now. 'Don't mind my brother, he's got no manners.' She grabbed Sara's hand and led her past Reece into the house. 'No coffee either, but at least I can do something about that.'

Kath stayed long enough to pour the coffee and unload the contents of two large shopping bags into the refrigerator. Then she took a last swig from her mug, professed herself delighted at having met Sara and apologised for having to run.

'Later, sis. I'll come by and pick Trader up this evening if that's okay.' Reece rose from the sofa and gave his sister a brief hug. 'Thanks for everything.'

'I just wish we weren't going away tomorrow. Perhaps I can stay behind a few days, Joe and the kids can manage on their own for a while...' Kath fisted her hand against

Reece's chest. Sara could never have done that with her own brother, and suddenly she envied Kath the careless gesture.

'Don't start trying to tear yourself in two again.' Reece held up an admonishing finger and Kath shrugged and nodded. 'If you can run some of that excess energy out of Trader this afternoon while we get sorted, that'll be fine.'

'Right. Later, then.' Kath grinned cheerily at Sara, and Trader followed her to the door with an air of almost palpable joy.

'At least Trader's found someone who's got their priorities straight.' Sara smiled, nodding at Kath as she jogged to her car, Trader trotting obediently behind her.

'Yeah.' Reece grinned. 'Cattle dogs can be a bit of a handful if they're not trained and exercised properly. Trader's ancestry is part dingo.'

'Yes, Simon told me. He said you helped him to train Trader.'

'Yep. He didn't have a clue where to start.' Reece shot her a quizzical look.

'No, he wouldn't. We didn't have pets at home. Too much mess.'

'That's a shame.'

'Yeah.'

Reece seemed to be waiting for Sara to elaborate, and when she didn't, he collected the empty coffee cups and put them into the dishwasher, leaving her to stare aimlessly out of the window. This sitting in one place, waiting to find out what someone else was going to do next, was the downside of being rescued.

'Right, then.' Reece obviously had a plan, even if she didn't. 'I expect you'll want to wash off some of that dust.' He turned, without waiting for her assent, and disappeared into the hallway. The only option available was to follow him.

'This is your room.' He flung one of the doors open and walked inside. 'The shower's through there, and Kath's left some things for you, so I hope you'll have everything you need.'

The room was bright and welcoming. Clean, cool shades of cream and green that just demanded you stay a while and relax. On the wide bed was a small pile of clothes, neatly folded. Next to it were towels and a small wicker basket containing soap, shampoo, toothpaste and some packages wrapped in paper. A large bunch of flowers sat on the table next to the bed, strange, brightly coloured blooms mixed with others that were more familiar to Sara.

This was a safe place, an oasis, where she could wash off the dust and sweat of the road. She couldn't accept it. She needed to stand on her own two feet. Make her own decisions.

'This is my guest room. It's yours for as long as you want it. At least until Simon gets out of hospital.'

From what Reece had said, that was going to be more than a week. 'I really can't impose. I'm very grateful for everything you've done already…'

'And what? Do you know anyone else here?'

No one. Apart from Simon, Reece was the only person who even came close to being a friend. 'I can book into a hotel. Near the hospital.'

'What, with Trader? Even if you find somewhere that'll take him, he'll get bored and tear the place apart.'

He had a point. 'Perhaps you wouldn't mind taking him. Just for a while, until I get something sorted.'

Reece rolled his eyes. 'Right. So I get to do a full day at the surgery then come home and take him out for a couple of hours to work off his excess energy. Anyway, what kind of person takes a mate's dog in and sends his sister to a hotel?'

Sara's hand flew to her mouth. 'I'm sorry. I didn't mean to…'

'Impose? You already said that. And you're not. You'll have to fend for yourself while I'm at work, but treat this place as your own.' He looked at his watch. 'It's half past ten now…an hour's drive to the hospital… We can catch our breath, have something to eat and be with Simon by lunchtime. What do you say?'

'That sounds wonderful. Thank you.' If she was going to stay here, she may as well do it gracefully. Her mother had told her that. Whatever you do, do it gracefully. Sara had been berated too many times for almost never following that advice.

'Good. Shall I call Simon, let him know that we're here, or would you like to?' He nodded at the phone extension next to the bed.

'I'd like to if that's okay.'

'Of course.' In one fluid movement he caught her hand, and Sara felt her cheeks redden. He produced a pen, pulling the cap off with his teeth in a gesture that was oddly almost piratical, and wrote on her palm. 'Here's the number. It's the main switchboard, but if you ask for Simon, they'll put you through to his room. Tell him that you and Trader are staying here.'

'Yes. I will. Thank you, Reece.' There was something else that she needed. The thought that Gran might have somehow heard about the fires was thudding at the back of her skull, like a headache about to happen. 'Would it be okay if I used your phone to call England?'

'Of course. Call whoever you want, you don't need to ask.'

'Thanks. I'll just be quick…'

He dismissed the notion with a weary gesture. 'Take as long as you like.' Turning swiftly, he strode out of the room and closed the door behind him. Sara heard the sounds of his footsteps along the hallway and another door opened. A thud as his heavy boots were dragged off and hit the floor. Then silence.

# CHAPTER THREE

SARA had made her calls and taken a shower. She sat on the bed, wrapped in a towel, and forced herself to take a couple of deep breaths. Gran was okay, Simon was okay. It was going to be all right.

Kath had left T-shirts, sweatpants and a skirt with a drawstring at the top, which would pretty much fit any size, along with a pair of open sandals. There was also a cotton nightdress and a note, saying that she should call her and let her know if there was anything else she needed. Sara smiled. The resemblance in tone to Reece's, kind but brooking no argument, was striking.

She dressed in her own jeans and one of Kath's T-shirts, and padded barefoot along the hallway and into the open-plan living area. Reece's car was still parked out front, but the house was silent and there was no sign of him outside on the veranda either. She took a deep breath. She knew exactly where he was, and it was the last place that she wanted to have to go and find him.

The door was slightly ajar, and she tapped on it nervously. Not a sound. Frowning, Sara cautiously craned her neck around the door to see inside.

He was lying on the bed, fast asleep. His boots, jeans and heavy shirt had been slung in the corner in the approximate direction of the laundry basket. It was as if he'd stripped down to his boxer shorts and then lain down, thinking just to close his eyes for a few moments, until it was time to move again.

His skin was smooth, golden. One arm thrown out to the side and the other rested across his chest. Sara caught her breath and for the first time allowed herself to stare at Reece. He looked so peaceful. The temptation to join him there on the bed, feel the steady, reassuring swell of his chest against her cheek, was almost irresistible.

*Stop this!* Peaceful he might be, but that wasn't what was freezing her to the spot. He was so beautiful. The snapshots that she'd already dared to glimpse—his chin, his brow—were nothing in comparison to being able to look for as long as she liked at the whole thing.

*Just a moment more.* One minute, to fantasise that she wasn't who she was, and he didn't live ten thousand miles away from where she had to be in another couple of weeks. It didn't work, and a minute wasn't enough. Sara drew back, and headed for the kitchen.

She'd made coffee for herself and sat in one of the wicker chairs on the patio with a book from the stack on the breakfast bar. She'd reckoned that she ought to wake him, and then chickened out and read another couple of chapters. Finally she decided that food would probably do the trick.

The amount of chopping, clattering and general commotion that it took before she heard his footsteps in the hallway attested to how tired he'd been. As did the fact that he was still half-asleep and had clearly forgotten that having company generally meant you didn't walk around the house half-naked. Sara concentrated on not slicing her finger along with the vegetables on the chopping board. She'd already seen what Reece had to offer, and there was no point in staring at what she couldn't have.

'Ready for something to eat?' She flung the words over

her shoulder and then gave in to the inevitable and looked in his approximate direction.

'Uh? How long have I been asleep?' He ran his fingers backwards through his hair in a lame effort to tame it a little.

'It's two o'clock.'

'What?' He straightened, suddenly seeming to come to. 'We should be at the hospital by now. Sara, I'm sorry. Why didn't you wake me?'

'Because you were asleep. How do you like your steak?'

He stared at her as if she had just landed in his kitchen from outer space. 'What?'

'Kath left some steak in the fridge. I hope you weren't planning on saving it for anything else?'

'No...no, of course not. What about Simon?'

'I called him and told him we'd be with him later on this afternoon.'

He grinned. It was the kind of easy, open grin that melted your heart, set it sizzling like butter in a pan. 'How is he?'

'He says he's fine. I'd like to see for myself, though.'

'Yes, we'll go as soon as we've eaten.' He tried to see what she had on the cooker. 'What's that you've got there? Smells great.'

Sara stepped in front of it. 'Wait and see. Are you hungry?' She was getting a crick in her neck. Fixing her gaze on his face, not allowing it to wander down to his chest, to the tiny line of sun-bleached hairs that disappeared into the waistband of his shorts, was making her jaw throb.

He grinned. 'I could eat a horse.'

'Bad luck, then. That's not on the menu. You've got ten minutes to have a shower if you want to.' Sara hoped that was enough of a hint to get out of her hair and stop distracting her. Maybe put some clothes on.

'Oh. Yeah, thanks.' One hand wandered to his chest and stayed there, as if he had only just realised that he had no shirt on. He turned quickly, and Sara allowed herself just enough of a glance in his direction to confirm that the view from the back was as good as that from the front. 'Pink.'

'What?'

'The steak. Pink but not too bloody, thanks.' He threw the words over his shoulder and disappeared.

He was back in five minutes, thankfully wearing a clean pair of cargo pants and a shirt, his short hair already half-dry. Banished once more from his own kitchen, he busied himself with laying the table in a shaded part of the veranda.

Sara laid his plate down in front of him and he grinned appreciatively.

'Looks good! If I'd been awake, I would have thrown myself in between you and the cooker.'

'In case my cooking's like Simon's?'

'Yeah.' He waited for her to sit down, and cut into his steak. 'This is just perfect.'

Steak with a black pepper sauce, potato gratin and green beans. Nothing fancy, but all done from scratch. 'Good. Thanks.'

'I could get used to this.' He tried the potatoes and nodded with approval. 'Obviously Simon missed out on the family cooking lessons.'

'Yes. Missed out on a lot.' Sara stopped herself. She didn't want to say anything to Reece that Simon wouldn't want him to hear. 'How long have you known him?'

'Ten years. He was working on the architect's plans for an extension to the hospital where I was working. Kath was there to meet me, and he tried to chat her up in the canteen.' Reece was grinning.

'So you found my brother trying to hit on your sister…' Sara laughed. 'How did that go?'

'Oh, pretty much as expected. I thumped my chest and growled a bit, and Kath kicked me under the table. Simon had told her that he was only just off the plane, and before I knew what had hit me, she'd roped us both in for a trip up to Sydney with her friends.'

'And did Simon and Kath ever…?' Sara waved her hand to indicate whatever it was that might have happened between the two of them.

'Nah. Kath's interest was purely humanitarian. We've both been in that situation enough times—new place, no friends—and she was just trying to make him feel at home.' He grinned. 'Kath does that.'

Reece did too. He'd taken her in without a second thought. 'Thank you. For looking after him.'

Reece gave her the smallest of nods in acknowledgement. 'So what about you?'

'Me?'

'Who looks after you?'

The question floored her for a moment and she stared at Reece, not sure quite how to answer. 'No one.'

'Surely there must be someone.' Reece was gazing at her intently and Sara felt her cheeks flush. 'Or haven't you told Simon about him yet?'

Suddenly, and quite unaccountably, she felt the need to defend herself. As if being single made it okay for her to have looked at Reece and wanted him, even if it was impossible, and she'd rather be dangled over a tank of hungry sharks than admit it.

'There's nothing to tell.' There was no time for a man in her life. When she wasn't working, Gran took up all of her spare time. A man couldn't be expected to stay with a woman who could only give him about five minutes of her undivided attention per day. 'There's been no one since before my mother died. And Simon's my only close family.'

Apart from Gran. Simon seldom asked about her, probably assuming that she still lived independently, and Sara didn't dare tell him any different until she could be more sure of his reaction. She could just about understand him staying away when their mother had been ill, but if he acted the same way with Gran, Sara would never be able to forgive him. And if Simon wasn't to know just yet, then telling Reece would be foolish.

They ate in silence for a while. 'Simon talked a lot about going home when your mother was ill.' Reece had clearly been giving some consideration to which bombshell to drop next.

'Did he?' Sara couldn't conceal her surprise. Simon had pretty much covered everything he'd had to say to her in one line of an email. He wasn't coming back. It would be hypocrisy to do so when his mother hadn't spoken to him for more than ten years.

'Perhaps he's been saving it. Until he sees you.'

'Maybe.' Maybe not. The last two years had been tough. First her mother had been diagnosed with cancer, and then her grandmother had fallen and broken her leg. Sara had given up her job, her home and, one by one, most of her friends in order to move back to her mother's house to take care of them both. She had never quite understood why Simon had stayed away.

'Give it time.'

'I thought I'd done that already.'

'Then give it some more.' He was holding her in his gaze. It felt almost as if he was cradling her, keeping her from any harm.

'Yeah, I suppose so.' She may as well say it. He'd obviously heard most of it from Simon already. 'I don't want you to think that it was all Simon's fault. Mum wasn't the easiest of people to live with. We each dealt with it differently. I gave in to her on the things that didn't matter and held out for the things that did. But Simon couldn't do that. They used to have the most awful rows.'

Reece nodded her on. He seemed to understand that she both wanted and needed to say this to someone. And he was all she had right now.

'It all came to a head when Simon said that he wanted to travel for a year after he'd done his degree in architecture. Mum had been pushing him away for years and then when he did leave she was so angry with him that she never mentioned his name again, even when she was dying.'

'Simon told me that your father leaving had a pretty big impact on her.'

'I don't remember that. I was just a baby.' Gran had told her about it, though. 'I'm told she just shut herself off from everyone, became totally focussed on showing that she was better off without him. She threw herself into work and built up a successful company from nothing. She used to say all the time that my father was unreliable and weak…' Too much information, perhaps.

'And that's what she said about Simon too?'

'Yes.' It felt good to be able to say it, even if it was hard. Sara swallowed down the lump in her throat. 'It's not true, though, is it?'

'No. That's not the friend I know.' The look in his eyes was almost unbearable. Liquid blue, as if she could somehow plunge into his world. Luxuriate in the safety of those cool, soothing waters. 'And you and Simon kept in touch. That has to say something, doesn't it?'

'Yeah. Not sure what…but, yes, it says something.'

He seemed to realise that she'd had enough, and that she couldn't talk about this any more. He nodded towards her plate. 'Eat. It's been a long day already, and it's not over yet. And this is too good to waste.'

'Thanks. There are some more potatoes in the kitchen if you want them. I always make too much.' She reached for his plate, but he was already on his feet.

'I'll go. You want some?'

'No, I'm fine with this, thanks.' Sara went back to her food, smiling as she heard the sound of a pan being scraped from the kitchen. She loved cooking, and having someone with appetite enough to scrape the pan was a welcome novelty.

'Do you like Australia?' When he returned to the table, he seemed as intent as Sara was on lightening the mood.

'I love what I've seen so far.' She shrugged. 'Simon and I have been keeping ourselves to ourselves since I arrived. You and Kath are the first real Australians that I've met.'

'Well, I hope we've not let the team down.' He grinned at her then looked at his watch. 'We'll get going as soon as we've finished lunch. Simon will be wanting to see you.'

# CHAPTER FOUR

AS FAR as appearances went, they'd fallen effortlessly into an easy routine. Up early so that Reece could do the forty-kilometre round trip to drop Sara at the nearest station before he went to work. Catching the train into Melbourne to spend time with Simon, then shopping and a tram ride back to Flinders Street Station, and home to cook for Reece.

The truth was a little different. Waking early and wondering if Reece was awake yet. Imagining the lazy flutter of his eyelids followed by the first sight of those clear, almost iridescent pools of blue. Three early nights in a row to escape the magnetic pull, which seemed to grow stronger as the sun fell in the sky and the moon rose.

The smile she liked best, held tight in her imagination during the day, was the one he gave her when he arrived home each evening. Today it was broader, more expectant, as if Reece had a surprise for her. 'We're going for a day trip tomorrow.'

'Really? Aren't you working?'

'No. It's Saturday tomorrow, in case that had escaped your notice. I've swapped shifts with one of the other doctors in the practice, and I have three days off.'

Something about the tone of his voice told Sara that he'd done that for her and she flushed with pleasure. 'That's great. So where are we going?' The distance to the local shops and the station was almost enough to be called a day trip at home.

'We're going to Simon's place.'

'The authorities have issued the all-clear?' She always waited until Reece got home so that she could check the news reports with him, telling herself that he could explain the things she didn't understand. But in truth she'd been living in a bubble, cushioned in his world, and now reality was calling. Earth to Sara. Time to wake up now, and get to grips with life.

'Yes. There are no more fires in that area now, and it's safe to return.'

'And the house? Do you know what's happened to the house, Reece?'

He shook his head. 'The fire went through that area, but I haven't been able to find out what happened to Simon's house.' His look of frustration told her that he'd tried. 'The house is surrounded by grassland, and there aren't too many trees on the property. The worst fires didn't get that far so there's a good chance that it's not badly damaged.'

He was giving her as much encouragement as he could, but he couldn't tell her what she wanted to hear. But at least she wouldn't have to wait too long to find out. 'Thank you. That sounds promising.'

'I found out where Simon's car is as well. We can pick it up on the way, it'll give you some mobility.'

Slowly the bonds that tied her here were unravelling. A car. And if everything went well, a house to live in too. For one brief moment Sara wished that Simon's house was somehow uninhabitable, and then cursed herself for her petty selfishness. 'So Trader and I might be out of your hair, then.'

'No. I said a day trip. You can't go back there.'

'Why not? If the fire's already been through, then there's

no more danger, is there?' The thought of a lonely house, in a blackened landscape, frightened her. Served her right. How could she have even thought about the possibility of a problem at Simon's house, however small and easy to fix, just so she could stay on here?

'That's not the point. We'll go back to the house, find out what's happened and salvage what we can. Then we come back here.'

He was giving her orders. She'd had enough of those from her own family, and Reece wasn't going to start that with her. He was about to turn away when she reached forward, catching the sleeve of his shirt. 'I'm grateful for everything you've done, but I can make my own decisions.'

'Not with this, Sara.'

'I'm not afraid.' Okay, so she was afraid. But she wasn't about to give Reece any more reasons to keep her here. 'If the house is okay, I'll stay there.'

'Right. So you know where to go to get petrol for the car, do you? Or where to get food if the local store is closed? The power's almost certainly off, so you'll have no running water, and you can't rely on the phone working either. What happens if you have an accident when you're on your own up there?' The tension lines had reappeared around his jaw, and his eyes flashed warning signals.

Trader slunk past them and out onto the veranda. He at least knew when to fold with Reece, but Sara wasn't ready to throw in her hand yet.

'Stop trying to frighten me, Reece. Lots of people will be going back to their homes. Why can't I be one of them?'

'Because you're alone. And you're not used to the terrain here, or the dangers. The emergency services have enough to do at this time of the year, without having to keep tabs on you.'

'So I'm a liability?' His words had stung her. He made

her sound like the kind of person who just did as she pleased and let other people pick up the pieces.

'You will be if you go back to the house. Simon would be the first to agree with me.'

'I imagine he would. Simon isn't my keeper, you know.' Sara felt herself flush. She was being unfair and Reece probably knew it just as well as she did.

Her outburst shocked them both to silence for a moment. When he spoke, Reece's voice was suddenly calm. 'You've been under a lot of stress, Sara.'

If he only knew. 'Don't patronise me.'

'I'm not patronising you. I'm asking you to stay here.'

There was an urgency in his tone that told her this was more than just a decision based on common sense. More than just a friend of the family, who was looking out for her safety. She should put a stop to that one right now. 'What for?'

Before she could take another breath, he had looped his arms around her waist, pulling her hard against his body. Before she could get used to the jelly-legged, head-swimming sensation that having him close to her produced, he was kissing her.

Reece knew he shouldn't be doing this. She was his friend's little sister. She was a guest in his house. She was also irresistible, and she'd pushed him too far.

She tasted sweet, with a tang of the chilli tomatoes that were simmering on the cooker. Yielding and yet fiery all at the same time, and he wanted to explore both of those options. Her body pressed against his, her fingers leaving trails of pure, excruciating pleasure. He took his mouth from hers, just for one moment, to allow himself to catch his breath, and a little sigh escaped her lips. He caught it in another kiss.

He backed her against the refrigerator door and she shivered slightly as her bare shoulders touched the cool surface, grinning upwards and reaching for him again. Pulling his head down towards hers, for one more kiss, this time her eyes open and staring into his. Dark and full of things that he wasn't sure he wanted to know about but simply couldn't resist.

There were about a million reasons why he shouldn't be doing this, but right now he couldn't think of any of them, because Sara was unbuttoning his shirt. Her fingertips found his skin and he gasped. She raked one nail gently across his chest and he felt his whole body shake.

A fridge magnet clattered to the floor and his itinerary for next week fluttered after it. No problem there. The foreseeable future had just changed.

'Kiss me again, Reece.'

He obeyed willingly, and she rewarded him by sliding her hands upwards, across his shoulders. A little sigh, and a shudder of pleasure that reverberated against his own aching body.

The phone rang.

No way! The sky could be falling in around their ears as far as he was concerned. He was busy.

The answering-machine kicked in. *'Reece. Pick up. It's an emergency.'*

They both froze. 'Go and get the phone.' She pushed him away from her, and Reece turned and snatched the handset from its cradle.

'This had better be good…'

It was good, all right. Or bad, whichever way you wanted to look at it. By the time he'd finished taking the message from his surgery, Sara had turned and was busying herself at the cooker.

'You have to go?' She'd clearly been listening to his side of the conversation, even though her back was to him.

'Yeah. I'm sorry, Sara.'

'What for?' She turned her eyes on him, dark and suddenly thoughtful. The moment had been well and truly shattered.

'For starting something I can't finish.' Reece wasn't sure whether the apology was for the starting part or the not finishing, but he could keep that open for the time being. 'One of my patients needs a home visit.'

'Would you like me to come along? Perhaps I can help.' She had already clapped the lid onto the saucepan and taken it off the heat, and was untying the strings of the butcher's apron that she wore. A trace of regret tingled through Reece's already inflamed nerve endings. He'd been looking forward to getting her out of that apron himself.

He forced his attention back to her question. Doubting her judgement had already gone down badly once tonight, and anyway he wanted her with him. 'Yes. That would be great. Thanks.'

They drove in awkward silence. Reece was used to being flung together with people and then letting go. The feeling that Sara might be ready to stand on her own two feet now, and that it was him who wasn't ready to let go, was unfamiliar and vaguely unsettling. When she finally did speak, her tone was measured.

'So what's the matter with the patient you're going to see?'

'Two-year-old child. Feverish, vomiting, listless.'

'Probably just a stomach bug, then.'

'Probably. Just as well to make sure, though.'

'Yeah. Absolutely.' She seemed to relax back into her seat slightly. 'Do you do this kind of thing a lot?'

He smiled at her. 'What, visit patients? All the time.'

'No, I meant get called out in the evenings.'

'Sometimes. We're pretty busy at the moment. And I'm a doctor in a semi-rural practice. When you're part of a community like this, the lines between off duty and on call tend to get a little blurred.'

'I imagine it has its compensations.'

It did. Knowing all his patients by their first names. Not being the 'new guy' who was just about to leave anyway. But it made him feel uncomfortable as well. He functioned better when he wasn't tied to one place.

'I said that I imagine it has its compensations.' Her voice cut through his reverie.

'Yeah, I suppose...' The possibility of staying put for long enough to find out was the one thing that Reece never talked about. The one part of his life that wasn't up for grabs. 'Yes, it does.'

The atmosphere in the car had turned from awkward to impossible, and Sara was glad when Reece turned into a driveway and drew up outside a large, sprawling house. As soon as he had grabbed his bag and got out of the car Reece was looking forward, though, on to the next thing. He was about as capable of hanging onto the past, even the very recent, mind-blowing past, as she was of growing wings and flying.

The front door opened before they got to it, and a young woman about Sara's age was standing at the threshold. Reece motioned Sara inside, introducing her briefly, and she followed him through to a child's bedroom.

'What's the matter, Ava?' He knelt down next to the child, who was whimpering fretfully.

'He's been sick. And he's feverish.'

'Any bites?'

'I don't think so.'

'Okay, let's take a look at him.' Reece turned to open

his bag, drawing out a pair of surgical gloves, and Sara kept her eyes on the child. She'd heard those high, keening cries before, but it could well be nothing. Leaning forward, she brushed one finger against his hand. Cold, even though the boy's flushed cheeks attested to him having a high temperature. Then she saw it.

'Reece. He has neck retractions.' She'd seen that rictus arching before too. She just hoped that Reece would react a little better to the suggestion than the doctor back in London had a few months ago. That time, a child had almost died before the doctors had accepted that Sara was right.

His gaze met hers and he nodded slightly. He'd got the message. 'Has he been arching his back, Ava? Throwing his head backwards?'

'Yes, a little. He's been wriggling around, he's not very comfortable at all.' Ava was looking back and forth between Sara and Reece, questions in her eyes.

'Okay, Ava. Come over here and let Reece take a look at him.' He had heard what she had to say and there was no more that she could do. A paramedic deferred to a doctor, that was the way things worked. Sara guided Ava over to a chair in the corner of the room and knelt down on the floor next to her.

The boy whimpered as Reece examined him. 'He's been like this all evening,' Ava confided to Sara. 'What's the matter with him?' Ava's instinct was telling her that something was badly wrong with her son, and that was just as telling as the indications that Sara had seen for herself.

'We don't know yet. But Reece will find out.' She wanted to tell Ava that her son was okay, but she knew better than to lie in this situation. She also knew better than to say the word 'meningitis' until there was a fuller diagnosis. Instead, she took Ava's hand, waiting while Reece worked.

'I think you're right, Sara. Call an ambulance—the

phone's in the hall.' He had made a careful examination of the boy and now he threw the instruction at her over one shoulder.

'What's the number?'

'Three zeros. We're at 211 Flowers Road.' Reece turned to Ava, who was now shaking visibly. 'You were right to call me, Ava. Now I'm going to tell you exactly what's happening and I want you to listen to me carefully.'

Sara hurried into the hallway and stabbed at the numbers. Quickly she reeled off the information that was asked of her, giving Reece's name as the doctor in attendance.

'They said twenty minutes.' Sara had no idea about whether that was a good response time or not. Out here the distances were so much greater and while there was not so much traffic for an ambulance to negotiate, everything was so much further apart.

'Good.' Reece looked at his watch. 'They'll be making good time if they get over here so soon. I'll write a letter for you to take with you, Ava. Where's Dan?'

'Over at his folks' place, helping with the vines.' Ava shrugged miserably. 'They're pretty busy right now.'

'All right, I'll give them a call and get them to find him. Don't worry, Ava, he'll be here.' He laid his hand on Ava's arm and she looked up at him gratefully.

'Thanks, Reece. If he's not back…'

'If he's not back by the time the ambulance gets here, we'll wait and send him on after you. Don't worry.'

By the time the ambulance arrived, Reece had written detailed notes and Sara had been sent to pack a few things for Ava so she could stay the night at the hospital. Ava sat with her son, never taking her eyes off him, as if by sheer force of will she might make him better. Maybe she could. Sara had seen stranger things.

Ava's husband arrived just as the ambulance crew were

settling their patient into the back of the vehicle. As Dan got out of his van, Reece caught his arm, saying something to him, his insistent stance demanding that the man listen before going to his wife and son. Then he let him go, and the family was swiftly installed in the back of the ambulance, ready to leave.

Reece stood, his hands in his pockets, watching the ambulance disappear. It was almost as if it carried his own family.

'He'll be okay.' Sara wanted to touch him, but didn't dare. After what they'd done this evening, no touch from her could be construed as pure consolation. And what they'd both wanted to do was hovering between them now, like a wayward genie that had popped out of a bottle and refused to be crammed back into confinement again.

'Yeah. I hope so. That was a good spot there, Sara.' He said the words awkwardly, as if even that might be construed as being inappropriate.

'Thanks. For listening to what I said.'

'Why shouldn't I?'

She shrugged. 'Oh, you know. Doctors don't always listen to paramedics.'

'A good doctor listens to everyone.'

'Yeah. Good doctors do that.'

He grinned, dipping his head slightly in a gesture of acknowledgement. In the last two hours they'd gone from housemates to almost-lovers and now they were colleagues. And colleagues seemed to be the only one of the three where they both knew what to do and how to act. Maybe, from here, they could work their way through to being friends, so that when the time came for them to part, they could both do it well.

It sounded like a plan, anyway. It was the only one that Sara had, so it had better work.

# CHAPTER FIVE

REECE was gratified to find that when Sara climbed into his SUV the following morning she pointedly did so without her large leather handbag slung across her shoulder. The few clothes that she had were still back in his guest room, and when he offered her his set of keys to Simon's house, she had waved them away. He was slightly ashamed at the swell of pleasure that it gave him to pocket them.

There was another battle to face, though, and that was the one that had been raging within himself. They'd been studiedly polite with each other throughout their meal last night, as if that was going to somehow erase the softness of her lips, make him forget how good she smelled and tasted and felt. And after she'd conjured up an urgent excuse for an early night out of nowhere, he'd found his own bed a little too large and much too lonely.

Fair enough. If that was what she wanted, then he would do nothing to make her feel uncomfortable. Restraint was the watchword for today.

Trader was about as jittery as he was, seeming to understand that they were on their way home, his tail thumping rhythmically against the back seat of the SUV as they drove.

'It looks…okay. Does it look okay?' Sara was peering out of the window intently.

'It looks fine. The fire didn't even get this far.' They still had over an hour's drive in front of them and she was nervous already. She'd start to see the devastation soon enough, and Reece knew she would deal with the reality much better than she would her own fears and imagination.

'No.' She seemed to settle a little. 'I'm glad it didn't reach that house over there, it looks like a nice place. The owners must be relieved.'

He grinned. Sara's glass always seemed to be half-full, even if it was with someone else's good fortune. 'Do you like it here?' He'd intended to change the subject, ease both their nerves, but as soon as the question had been asked, Reece realised that it mattered to him. It mattered a great deal.

'I love it. It's so…' She seemed lost for words for a moment. 'I feel free here. As if I can see a long way into the distance.'

'Yeah? Not so much in the way, I guess.' His fingertips were tingling.

'It's not that. It's the light. So clear, I feel as if I could almost touch it.' She was smiling now and it was hard to keep his eye on the road.

'Not as exciting as London, though.' He shouldn't press the point. He shouldn't be wondering what she might say if he asked her to stay on for a little while.

She shrugged. 'London's different. It's got a lot going for it, and so has this place.' She seemed to be thinking about something. Maybe weighing up the pros and cons. Reece almost held his breath. 'You must have seen pretty much all of Australia.'

'Not all of it. Quite a lot, though.'

'But you're home now?'

The question took him by surprise. Reece tried to decide where exactly might be classified as home, and came up blank. 'Not really. I came here to be with Kath. She had postnatal depression after she had her second child and she and Joe needed some support.'

'She's better now?' She swung round to look at him.

'Yeah. Took a while, but she's fine.'

'Does that mean you'll be moving on, then?'

Reece reckoned up the time in his head. 'I've lived in the same place for two years and three months now. That's pretty much a record for me.'

She laughed, shaking her head. 'All right, then, what's your favourite part of Australia?'

'Can't say, really. Everywhere has something to recommend it.'

'Hmm. Yes, you're right. There are so many wonderful things in the world.'

She had a knack of making things wonderful. After her first day in Melbourne she'd described her tram ride to Reece with such infectious enthusiasm that he'd thought that the next time he took that familiar route it would seem new and exciting. 'You must have travelled a bit. Europe's right on your doorstep.'

'Oh, nowhere, really. Italy…France.' She sounded almost wistful. As if somehow they were places that were out of her reach, although there was nothing stopping her now from going wherever she wanted. 'What about you?'

'New Zealand, of course. India, Indonesia, Japan…' He reeled off the list of countries and she laughed delightedly. 'I've not got as far as Europe yet, but I'll make it there one day.'

'You should.' That hint of sadness again, which was shaken off almost straight away. 'Simon said that you and Kath travelled a lot when you were young.'

'Yeah. My father was an entertainer, so we were on the move most of the time.'

'Really?' That touch of wonder again. 'What did he do?'

'He was a magician. He even had his own TV show.'

'What? So you know how to do magic tricks?'

Reece laughed. 'A few.'

'Show me!'

Suddenly a few simple conjuring tricks became a precious legacy from a childhood that had forced Reece to leave almost everything he'd cared about behind. 'I can't while I'm driving.' Reece wondered whether she was going to make him stop the car and produce a coin from her ear right this minute.

'Well, you can show me as soon as we get back to your place this evening.'

He grinned. His place this evening sounded like a promise with possibilities. 'You're on.'

The terrain was beginning to change. Yellow and green gave way to patches of burned-out land, and Sara stared out of the car window, trying to comprehend the vastness of it all. Great swathes of charred, black ground, the odd patch of untouched earth, which made the destruction wrought by the oncoming flames seem random and all the more chilling.

The smell of smoke still hung in the air, and she could glimpse the roof of Simon's house as Reece sped towards it. At least the place still had a roof. That seemed like a good sign, and she held onto it, not daring to ask Reece. He wouldn't lie, and for the next few moments, at least, hope was better than the uncertain truth.

The wooden outhouse, only fifty feet from the house, was an unruly pile of cinders with just a few charred structural beams still upright. The fire had taken the grassland around the property, but the house was untouched.

'Reece…' Sara couldn't help but reach across to him, and she felt his hand grab hers, holding it tight while he steered the SUV up the bumpy track towards the house with the other hand. 'Look, it's okay.'

'Yeah.' He sounded as relieved as she was, and Sara realised that he had shared her fears. 'Looks as if the fire was losing some impetus by the time it got here. The firebreak around the house was enough.'

'If you hadn't come for me…' Tears pricked at the sides of her eyes. Even though the house was untouched, Sara could only imagine the terror of being stranded there alone as the fire surrounded her.

'Don't think about that.' The car came to a halt outside the house and he turned, taking both her hands in his. 'It might be a bit of a mess inside, but don't worry about that. We can fix it.'

'Yes…yes, we can make it just the way it was before.'

He nodded. 'That's the spirit. Stay here for a moment with Trader while I go and check the place out.'

'I'll come with you…if that's all right.' Even though it went against all of her instincts, if Reece insisted she stayed here, she'd do it.

'Sure.' He reached into one of the compartments in the car door and drew out two pairs of heavy workmen's gloves, grinning as he handed her one. 'Whatever made me think you'd stay put?'

Trader, on the other hand, was told to stay and grudgingly lay down on the back seat of the car, his tail thumping out a message of rebellion. Reece caught Sara's gloved hand in his, whether as comfort or as a way of keeping her from straying she didn't know. She didn't much care. It was a world away from the way that their fingers had frantically twined together last night, and a welcome reassurance that today Reece could somehow make everything right.

Reece tested his weight on the boards of the veranda

before he let her follow him. Everything that he kicked or thumped with the heel of his hand was firm and solid.

'Looks as if Simon did a pretty good job when he designed this house. These fireproof boards have held up pretty well.' He gave the veranda one more kick to illustrate his point.

'I'm glad I wasn't here.' Sara looked at the blackened landscape and tried to imagine it burning. She couldn't. Some things were just beyond imagining.

His eyes were following the progress of a small flock of birds, dipping and wheeling in the distance over what was probably a source of either food or water. 'You did all the right things, Sara. Pulled the shutters down in case you had to stay. Packed up Simon's things in case you got the chance to go.'

'I don't know about that. I was pretty scared.' Perhaps she should have just left it. But she couldn't help wanting more from him.

'Anyone with an ounce of sense would have been. You handled yourself well.'

'Apart from locking us out of the house, that is.' Sara shrugged and turned away from him.

She heard his chuckle behind her. 'I'd have forgiven you anything at that point. You looked so cute in your jeans and your nightie. A bit like a wayward fairy who had lost her way in the bush.'

Sara heard the sound of the shutters as he pulled them up over the front door, and she turned, watching him. Waiting to see what he would do next, almost afraid of going into the house.

'It's a little stale in there.' He pushed the door open and the smell from the house hit her. A little stale didn't cover it. The place stank.

For a moment her courage failed her and Sara hesitated.

He seemed to understand, pulling off his glove and reaching for her, his fingers brushing the soft skin on the inside of her wrist. Sara thought she saw an echo in his eyes of the thrill that the contact gave her.

'Leave the door open. It'll air out.' He made no comment when Sara decided to follow him around the perimeter of the house, watching while he pulled the rest of the shutters up.

When he got to the back door, he unlocked it and propped it open to get a little more air into the house. By the time they had worked their way back to the front, the smell of smoke and decay from inside seemed to have lessened a little.

Everything inside looked tired and worn, from the onslaught of the smoke. Reece made for the kitchen, with Sara hard on his heels. She didn't need to follow him around any more, but somehow his bulk and the certainty of his movements were reassuring.

The fruit in the bowl was rotten and stinking. Sara left his side and inspected the food in the fridge, which was beginning to smell, a dried watermark on the floor from where it had defrosted.

'I'll go and get my tools from the car and see what I can do about fixing the front door.' He hesitated, silent questions in his eyes.

Sara nodded. He'd taken her the first few baby steps and she was ready to do this alone now. 'Thanks. I'll see what I can do about cleaning this mess up.'

He'd brought everything she needed. Waste sacks, cleaning sprays and even two large canisters of water, which he heaved from the car and rolled into the kitchen, telling Sara to go easy with it as it was all they had, apart from the drinking water they'd brought. She set about emptying the fridge and cleaning away the black dust that covered every exposed surface, while Reece clattered around at the front door.

When she wandered through to find him, not entirely satisfied that the kitchen was clean but confident that she'd got the worst of it, he'd almost finished with the door.

'What do you think? Once it's filled, sanded and painted, it'll hardly show.' He ran his hand across the wood he'd pieced into the doorframe where the lock was smashed, testing the alignment with his fingers.

'It looks great. It won't show at all.' She grinned at him and he nodded, seemingly now satisfied with his work.

'How are you doing?'

'I've pretty much finished in the kitchen. Have you got Simon's list?'

Reece pulled the list out of his pocket. 'There's the computer he uses for work and his back-up drives…I'll get those and see if I can clean up a bit in his office. Some bits and pieces from his wardrobe…' He twisted his wrist, flipping the sheet of paper towards her. 'Bring as much as you can fit into the car. We can wash clothes and bedding when we get them back home.'

Sara took the list without touching his fingers. 'Sure.' She'd given in to the need to touch him too much today already. Now that she was feeling stronger, her head was throbbing from trying not to think about how a comforting touch could so easily turn into a caress.

As soon as she had taken refuge in Simon's bedroom, Sara began to think more clearly. She simply couldn't give in to temptation where Reece was concerned. Ten thousand miles was nothing in comparison to the distance between their lifestyles. He was a free spirit, and she had made the choice to stay put and look after Gran.

She didn't regret it for a moment, but experience had taught her that it was better not to think about relationships.

If Tim, her last boyfriend, who had never gone anywhere unless absolutely necessary, reckoned that caring for her mother and grandmother had made her boring, then Reece wouldn't last ten minutes.

She sighed. Tim hadn't been that much of a loss anyway, she'd hardly missed him when he'd left. Reece would be, though. And what you didn't have, you couldn't miss.

She sank onto the bed, shrugging to herself. *So don't do it. Just don't. That's the easy way out of this.* Kissing goodbye to the thought of his caress might be the most obvious course of action, but it wasn't as easy as it sounded.

'Forget about that, there's work to do.' She muttered the words through gritted teeth and her body automatically obeyed. Sara opened the wardrobe and sorted clothes into neat piles on the bed. She went to the bathroom for Simon's shaving kit. Rummaging through the heavy workboots to find the soft-soled sneakers he'd asked for, Sara jagged her fingers on a sharp edge, right at the back of the wardrobe.

Investigating more closely, she drew out a large, metal banker's box, sliding it onto the carpet. It was heavy. Papers perhaps. If so, they should take these too. There was a lock on the box but it hung open, with two keys taped to the side, so whatever it was couldn't be private.

She opened the lid and found neat piles of papers and photographs. Her own face smiled out at her from a trip to France three years ago. Gingerly Sara picked up the stack of photographs, flipping through them. They were all of her, photos that she'd sent over the years. Postcards from when she'd been on holiday. Every single thing that she'd ever sent Simon.

Their mother was there too. Press cuttings from English papers that Simon must have had subscribed to. Articles about the company, even advertisements from the recruitment section. A page spread of their mother, accepting the

Public Relations Manager of the Year Award, carefully folded so that the creases in the paper didn't run across any of the photographs.

She jumped guiltily as Reece appeared in the doorway. 'Have you got any bags of clothes that I can pack around the computer to steady it in the car…?' He broke off as Sara looked up at him. Her bewilderment must have been written all over her face. 'What's the matter?'

'Nothing. Nothing. I…' She had no idea how she should react to this. She wanted to cry, but a lump of concrete in her chest seemed to be stopping her. 'Have you seen this box before?'

'No. Why?' He watched as she closed the lid of the box. She should leave it.

'Nothing. It doesn't matter.' She got to her feet and started to slide the piles of clothes into plastic sacks. Subject closed. It made no difference, anyway.

'Since it's nothing…' he walked into the room and sat down on the bed, watching her for a moment '…you won't mind if I look inside the box, then.'

# CHAPTER SIX

THE unfamiliar, awkward sensation of not knowing what to do next had turned Reece's hands into heavy, clumsy things that he didn't recognise. He'd been trying his best to give Sara the support she needed, balancing that with the space she wanted. But his instincts had been warring with his conscious mind for so long now that he couldn't be absolutely sure about his motives for anything any more.

She was obviously upset. She had that strange air of being just about to burst into tears, without actually doing so. And tears or not, he wanted to comfort her but he couldn't do that unless he knew what the matter was. An abrupt gesture of her hand indicated that he could do whatever the hell he liked, and Sara turned away from him.

'Did you know he had all this?' Finally she spoke.

'No. I didn't.' Reece could have guessed, though. He didn't have a box like this in the bottom of his own wardrobe but everything, every scrap of paper, every last memory of his own brother, still followed him wherever he went, stored in a large manila envelope.

'Why did he do it?' She was pacing now, and it was difficult to tell exactly who she was angry with. Perhaps she didn't even know. 'Why couldn't he have come back? Mum would have seen him at the end. I know she would, whatever she said.'

'I don't know. We all deal with things differently, Sara.'

'How hard would it have been just to make some sort of effort to see us, instead of locking us away in a metal box?' Swiping her hand across her face, she threw herself back down onto the bed next to him. 'I guess I didn't mean that.'

'I guess that you did, and I don't blame you.' She still wouldn't look at him, but her body seemed less taut now. 'Have you and Simon talked about your mother yet? Why he didn't come home?'

'No. I've been meaning to mention it, but…' She shrugged. 'I don't know if that's ever going to happen.'

Reece took a deep breath. He'd been keeping out of this, reckoning it was best to let Simon and Sara work things out between themselves, but now might be the time to revisit that assessment. 'You're more like him than I thought.'

It was deliberate provocation, and it worked. Better than he'd anticipated.

'What do you mean by that?' Her face flushed with anger.

'Simon walks away. It's what he does. If something's emotionally difficult then he'll let it slide. But you…' Reece decided to go for it. If Sara was half the woman he thought she was, she'd rise to the challenge. 'I had you down as being stronger than that.'

She stared at him, clearly not sure whether to take what he'd said as an insult or a compliment. 'I'm not…I'm not strong…'

'I think you're one of the strongest people I've ever met.' Her doubts about herself would have been almost laughable if they hadn't tugged so fiercely at his heart.

'So it's me that has to do all the running, is that what you're saying? Why can't Simon do something?'

'It's not fair, but that's how it is.' His words had a whiff of hypocrisy. 'Can I tell you something?'

She sensed his reticence, and it seemed to calm her. 'Yes, of course.'

Carefully, tentatively, he reached back into his past. 'It wasn't just Kath and I when we were kids. We had a brother.'

'Oh?'

'My mother died just after Kath was born. Dad remarried and my stepmother had a son, about my age. We grew up together and we were like brothers. I guess that travelling so much threw us together. It was me, Kath and Stuart, and we didn't need anyone else.'

She nodded for him to go on, resting her hand lightly on his.

'When I was fourteen, my dad and stepmum divorced.' He shrugged. 'She found him with one of the dancers from the show and walked out. I was confused and angry and I wouldn't speak to Stuart when he wanted to say goodbye. I didn't see him again.' He laid her hand back in her lap. It was okay. Really, it was.

'What I'm trying to say to you, Sara, is that families get split up for all sorts of reasons. People act badly. They make mistakes. I haven't seen Stuart for twenty years and I often wonder what became of him.'

She swallowed. 'Reece, I'm sorry...'

'It doesn't matter. I'm telling you this because you have a chance to mend things between you and Simon. If I had that chance with Stuart, I wouldn't waste it.'

She looked at him, wide-eyed and knowing. As if her gaze could pierce him, right to the heart. 'Have you ever tried to find him?'

'Yeah, I've tried. Sometimes I think that I'll go to a new town, pop into the local chemist and bump into him.' He shrugged. 'Not particularly likely, though.' Reece hadn't realised how much it would cost him to say that. How bad it felt to finally admit that he would probably never find his brother. He could feel himself beginning to shake and he got to his feet and walked over to the window, staring out at nothing in particular.

He felt her arm brush his. Whatever he was looking at out there, it seemed to have captured her attention too. 'I hope that someone's looking after Stuart. Being a friend to him, the way that you and Kath have been to Simon all this time.'

'Thanks. I hope so too.' He felt suddenly lighter. As if in trying to convince her that she was not alone, he'd finally convinced himself of that fact.

He had to make some space between them. If he didn't, he was going to do something stupid. Start believing that kissing her last night had been the sanest thing he'd ever done, and that he should repeat it. Up here, it would be nothing short of a miracle if the phone interrupted them.

'What do you think of this?' He turned quickly, and in the absence of anything else to busy himself with began to stack the piles of Simon's clothes into the case that lay open on the bed. 'We'll close the box up, lock it and take it back to my place for safekeeping. If the time comes when you and Simon want to look through it together, then it'll be there for you both.'

'Yes. Thanks, I'd like that.' She was wiping at the grime on her face with her fingers, producing a streaky effect. Not many women could have carried that off well, but somehow she looked just fine. Impish. Reece tried not to think about the mischief she could get up to, but it was too late. Desire had already ignited, deep in his gut.

'Okay, then. We'll pack the car, and then we can clean up before we get back on the road.'

'Wash?' Her face brightened. 'I thought the water pump wasn't working?'

'It isn't. But I've got some more water in the car.' He grinned at her obvious pleasure. 'One basinful each.'

'One basin is plenty.' She tugged at her T-shirt, now caked with soot. 'I'm glad now I took your advice and brought a change of clothes. This stuff gets everywhere.'

'And since we'll be more or less presentable, there are some nice wineries on the way back. Perhaps we can stop and I'll buy you a late lunch.' He might not be about to give in to his other fantasies, but they had to eat.

'No.'

Reece felt a trickle of cold sweat down his back. Perhaps he'd gone too far after all.

She laughed. The sound of her laugh was like the gentle patter of rain on leaves, breaking a long, hard drought. 'It's my shout. You've been so good to me, Reece, the least I can do is buy lunch.'

'Right. Fair enough.' He could handle that. 'Never turn a lady down when she's paying.'

Reece had driven past three wineries, which for some reason weren't good enough, and settled on a fourth, turning into a wide driveway and parking the car in a space surrounded by vines. They walked together through the light, airy restaurant space and out onto a wide, shaded veranda at the back.

'Is this okay?' He scanned the space, still apparently making up his mind about whether his choice was the right one.

'It'll do.' Sara sat down at the nearest table before he got the chance to spend another ten minutes deciding which had the best view. Reece hadn't initially struck her as the kind of person that it was all that easy to tease, but he was looking distinctly uncomfortable at the moment. 'It's lovely. Sit down before you take root there.'

Once she'd looked at the menu and pronounced it varied enough for her taste, declared the view across the vineyard delightful and confirmed herself to be not too hot or too cold, he loosened up a little. Sara stretched her legs out in front of her, slipping her feet out of her sandals and relishing the feel of the sun on her toes.

'So are you going to show me some of those magic tricks? Or do you need special equipment?'

'They're called props. And, no, you don't need any, because it's really and truly magic.' A grin hovered on his lips.

'Go on, then.'

He produced a coin from his pocket, holding it up for her to examine and then closing his fingers around it. 'I expect you've seen this one before. Keep your eyes on my hand.'

'I'm watching you carefully.' Sara fixed her eyes on the hand he held the coin in.

He chuckled, blew on his hand and then opened it, splaying his fingers wide to show her that the coin was now gone. Then he reached forward, a slight tremor in his fingers as they brushed her ear, making her flush red.

The coin clattered to the floor. His gaze was all for her now, and hers for him.

'Astonishing.'

He smiled, leaning across the table towards her. 'You missed the bit at the beginning. When I told you to watch carefully, I'd already switched the coin to my other hand.'

'I'll look a bit closer next time. Aren't you supposed to give the coin to me so I can check it's the same one?'

'Yep.' He didn't move. The magic going on here was the real kind, no smoke or mirrors. One touch of his gaze, a slight movement of his hand towards hers, and she could feel that slightly giddy sensation of being lighter than air.

A waitress broke the spell, unloading two glasses of

wine and a platter of food from her tray. 'Hey.' She bent down and picked up the coin. 'Is this yours?'

Reece grinned up at her. 'Thanks. Belongs to the lady.'

'Ah, right.' She laid the coin on the table in front of Sara. 'Enjoy your food.'

'Thank you.' Sara surveyed the seafood platter. 'This all looks wonderful.'

The waitress grinned and nodded when she heard Sara's accent. 'There's a guestbook on the bar where you can write what you think of our wine.'

'Thanks, we will.' Suddenly it was *we* and not *I*. As if they really had somehow melded together for a moment, and it wasn't just an illusion brought about by the seductive heat in his eyes.

He seemed to feel it too. Spearing some of the best bits from the platter and reaching over to drop them on her plate. His fingers brushing against hers as they both reached for the bread at the same time. The sun, the breeze and Reece's easy, open smile were working on her heart. If she could talk to Simon, what other impossibilities might she accomplish? Today she could do anything. Just for today.

That evening, Reece sat in the visitors' lounge at the hospital, the newspaper folded in front of him, ignoring the partially completed crossword. He didn't have the heart for it at the moment. Sara had already been with Simon for an hour and a half and the debate over whether he had pushed her into this too soon or just encouraged her to do what she already knew was right wasn't going well.

He had positioned himself carefully so that he could see along the corridor that led to Simon's room. When he saw her, walking slowly, her face creased in that worried look that seemed almost a matter of habit when she thought no one was looking, it was all he could do not to jump to his feet and hurry to meet her.

'How did it go?' He tried not to make the question sound too insistent.

'Good. I said what I had to say, and Simon responded to it.' Suddenly she smiled, and Reece breathed again. It was like the sun rising over the hills, with its bright promise of a new day.

'That's great.' He wondered whether he should ask where things stood now and decided not to. It was enough that she was smiling. 'Would you like me to get you a drink, or do you want to go now?'

'Let's go.'

Reece stood and made to follow her towards the exit door, but she stopped suddenly, catching his arm. 'We're okay with things. I mean, more okay than we were. It wasn't easy, and Simon said a lot of things that I didn't particularly want to hear. They needed saying, though.'

'I'm glad. Things like this, you can't mend them in one go. All you can do is make a start.'

'And we made a good one. Thanks, Reece. For your advice.'

Her words stung. He'd advised her to talk honestly with Simon, but he hadn't been entirely honest with her. The things he'd done today, getting close to her, trying to lift her spirits, hadn't been entirely selfless. They were the things he'd been longing to do. His motives had seemed solid enough at the time, but in retrospect they didn't stand up to very much scrutiny.

'Any time.' He ignored the hypocrisy of that statement too. This urge to be with her, all day and all night, wasn't appropriate either. She was a guest in his house, dependent on him, and she had a lot to cope with right now. She needed support, not someone else to mess with her head.

'Let's go home.' She stretched her arms out, working loose the tension in her shoulders.

'Yeah, it's been a long day. I'll pick up a take-out and a DVD rental on the way and we can just relax in front of the TV.'

She brightened immediately. 'Mmm. A shower and then food on the sofa with a film. Heaven.'

# CHAPTER SEVEN

A BRIGHT, clear dawn did little for Reece's sense of disappointment in himself. Sara had fallen asleep halfway through the film, and two hours later, when she hadn't stirred, he'd carried her through to her room. He'd resisted the temptation to change her into her nightdress, deciding that she'd be comfortable enough in her sweatpants and T-shirt, but he'd not been able to find a good reason not to take her socks off. And after the swell of longing that brushing her ankle with his fingers had engendered, even that had seemed like an unpardonable intrusion.

The morning found him staring uncertainly at the contents of the refrigerator. Since she'd been here, the plastic food containers that usually lay undisturbed at the back of the cupboard had migrated to the fridge. All of them contained something, and he had little idea what.

'What are you looking for?' Reece jumped guiltily as he heard her voice behind him.

'Not sure yet. I'll know when I see it.'

She laughed and Reece turned in surprise. As laughs went she had a great one, but it was always cut short, as if she'd remembered that there really wasn't much to laugh about. This one seemed to run its course.

'There's bread in the cupboard and some fruit sliced in the second container on the left. Juice in the door, and…'

She slid past him and flipped open a cupboard, reaching for a packet from the top shelf. 'Look what I got.'

'Ah! Coffee beans. I thought we'd be back to instant when the ground coffee Kath brought over ran out.' He saw that there was another, similar packet stowed away behind the first. 'And you stocked up.'

She grinned at him. 'From the state of your coffee grinder, it looked as if you hadn't used it for a while.'

'That bad, eh?'

'Nothing a hammer and chisel couldn't fix.' She was playful this morning, and it warmed Reece's heart to see her like this. It started him thinking about what she could so easily be if that nebulous, unknown burden that she seemed to carry around with her was lifted. 'Sit down. I'll make breakfast.'

'You don't need to do that…' She'd been cooking for him ever since she'd arrived here and Reece was painfully aware of the fact that he'd eaten better in the last week than he didn't know when.

'Sit.' She was irrepressible and quite irresistible. 'I don't want you messing up your own kitchen. You can do that when I'm safely out of the country.'

She made breakfast and Reece came back for seconds in what was becoming almost a private joke between them. 'I could get used to this, you know.' He leaned back in his chair, full and ready for the day. Usually he left the house hungry and stopped off at the coffee shop on his way in to work.

'Maybe you should.' Her dark eyes found his gaze, and for a moment the world seemed to open up, full of possibilities. 'It's just a matter of organisation. Keeping a shopping list.'

'Yeah. Guess so.' Reece had never made a shopping list in his life. Neither of his stepmothers or his father's live-in girlfriends had ever made shopping lists either, let alone keep stocks of food in the cupboards. It was one of the byproducts of living in a different place every couple of months. Learning the lesson about not getting too attached to anything or anyone. 'I never really thought…'

He'd never really thought about a lot of things. About the single flower, taken from the garden and put into a vase between them on the table. About the smell of home-cooked food and how that curled around his senses, welcoming him home in the evenings. How two chairs, tilted towards each other on the patio, were so much more sociable than straightening them neatly.

The phone shrilled from inside the house and Reece rose, hoping that it wasn't a call from the surgery. He had other plans for today.

It was Simon, and he sounded as cheerful as his sister did. 'Some of the guys from work are coming in this afternoon. We were thinking of watching the game together and I reckoned that Sara deserved a break.'

Simon was playing right into his hands. 'I can take her out somewhere.' He found himself lowering his voice conspiratorially.

'That would be great. Would you mind?'

'Of course not.' He ignored the chorus of voices at the back of his head. He was doing a favour for a friend. Where was it written that had to be an irksome duty?

'Yeah. There were loads of places I was hoping to take her, and she hasn't got to see any of them yet.'

'Okay.' There was one person who still needed to be convinced. He could drop Trader off at a neighbour's and have Sara all to himself for the day. 'Well, I'll leave it to you to persuade Sara that it's okay for her to take some time off today.'

* * *

The rest of the day was hers. And what a day it was. Sara supposed that Reece pretty much took these bright, clear days for granted, and that he took the feeling of freedom that they seemed to engender for granted too. She didn't. She was enjoying every moment of them.

'Where are we going again?'

'You'll see.' Reece seemed to be taking pleasure in the fact that she'd lost her bearings completely. 'Again.'

'Can't you show me on the map?'

'What for? I know the way.'

'I'm a tourist. I need a map.' She shot him a pleading look. 'Suppose…'

'Suppose what?'

He had a point. 'I don't know. Suppose anything. Suppose you got electrocuted in a freak lightning storm and lost your memory.'

'I'd look in my wallet for my address. Suppose you take the day off. Let someone else cover all the eventualities for a few hours.'

That generally wasn't an option, but since it was now, there was no real reason why she shouldn't take it. Sara settled back into her seat. 'Okay.' At first she'd hated being so dependent on Reece, having to trust him for practically everything. Some time over the last week, though, it had become suspiciously easy.

'Really?' As he raised one eyebrow, the car kicked down a gear, attacking the steep incline of the road as if it too didn't quite believe her but was pressing on regardless.

The road wound, climbing all the time through dense woodland. Sara caught glimpses of rolling hills, which Reece drove past without slowing, and Sara twisted in her seat, trying to get a better look. Finally he did slow, pulling into an off-road car park.

'Are we here, then?' Sara got out of the car before Reece had a chance to start the engine again.

'We're here. Would you like to go for a walk?'

'Thought you'd never ask.' The forest around them was spectacular. Massive trees, giant ferns. 'I've never seen anything like this before.'

He seemed pleased at the way she was looking around, drinking it all in. 'Put your boots on and we can explore a bit. How are you with heights?'

'Fine. As long as my feet are firmly on the ground.' Sara covered her discomfiture by opening the back door of the car and pretending to look for her walking boots.

Reece watched while she laced them up and caught up the daysack he'd brought along. 'Let's go this way, then.' He turned resolutely and started to make his way towards the far end of the car park, twisting round when he realised that Sara wasn't with him.

'What about this way?' She jerked her thumb towards the signpost that pointed towards the trail that wound upwards and disappeared amongst the trees.

He hesitated, and Sara leant back against the car, folding her arms. So what if she didn't like heights very much? She wouldn't be coming back here any time soon and she was determined to see everything while she had the opportunity.

'You might find it a bit…challenging.' He still seemed unsure.

'Good. I'm in a mood for a challenge.' She was used to planning the easiest possible way to do anything with Gran, and this felt like an opportunity to stretch her limbs.

He grinned broadly, striding back over to where she stood. 'Okay, then. A challenge it is.'

Reece took her hand, leading her along the trail. On one side of them the ground suddenly fell away, only a sturdy handrail and a couple of feet of ground between them and a dizzying drop. 'Okay?'

She gripped his hand tightly. 'I'm okay.' She took hold of the handrail, testing it, and when it didn't give she took a step forward. Not too bad. With Reece on one side of her and the railings on the other, she felt almost safe. Sara took another step and then let him guide her forward.

Awe took over from fear. On one side of them was the canopy of the forest. Below them was dense vegetation, with the tops of the trees and the sky above them. It was breathtaking.

Reece was at her side, keeping up a steady stream of information. He pointed out the tall mountain ash and the myrtle beech trees, the giant ferns and various mosses. Every part of this ancient, gigantic forest seemed to fascinate him as much as it did her. She let go of the handrail and fished in her bag for her camera.

'Stop a moment. I want to take a photo.' Before she had even thought what she was doing, she motioned him forward. 'Go and stand over there. I need something to show how big the trees are.'

'You go, then.' He took the camera from her. 'Or do you just want to stay here and I'll take one?'

'No, no, I want that big one over there.' Sara walked ahead of him to stand in front of the tree she wanted. Reece backed up to get as much as he could into the frame, and Sara smiled for the camera.

A few exchanged words with a middle-aged couple who were passing and he handed the camera over and came to join her, standing next to the balustrade. Sara inched closer and he put his arm around her.

'Beaut!' the woman exclaimed delightedly, and clicked the shutter. Sara grinned and heard the camera click again. 'Here you are, doll.' The woman came forwards and handed her the camera, smiling at them both. 'You make a lovely couple.'

Reece watched, amused, as Sara thanked the woman awkwardly and then reviewed the photos with shaking fingers. 'Don't we just.' She jumped as his lips brushed her ear, and then he drew back, letting her put the camera back into her bag.

They had explored the trail together, and then a longer trail, which wound through the forest floor. Sara held her breath as Reece pointed out a lyrebird, which took fright almost as soon as she caught sight of it and made for the safety of the undergrowth. They paused to stand beneath gigantic ferns that looked like something out of a set for a prehistoric movie.

Reece drove to the summit so she could get the best view of the densely wooded hills that surrounded them, and then came the long drive back down again, marvelling at the dark shapes of the trees against the sun, now falling towards the horizon.

'Did you like it?' They'd been almost silent in the car as Sara had determinedly tried to drink in every sight and sound of the day.

'Out of this world.' She laughed. 'Almost literally.'

He smiled. 'It's something else, isn't it? Makes you feel very small when you think that some of these trees have been growing for nearly four hundred years.'

'Do you think they'll be there in another four hundred?'

'Who knows? With a little luck, some good management and the will to do it. I hope so.'

'It matters, doesn't it?'

'Yeah. It matters.' He slowed the car, giving a cyclist who was freewheeling down the steep gradient a wide berth. Another car shot past them, and Sara stretched automatically to look in the rear-view mirror.

'Stop the car!'

He didn't ask why, just jammed his foot on the brake. As soon as the car skidded to a halt, Sara jumped out, running back up the road for all she was worth. She could hear Reece behind her, and by the time she got to the spot where she had last seen the cyclist, he was at her side.

'Over there. That car that overtook us must have just clipped him and sent him off the road.' He pointed to where the thin trails, left by the bicycle wheels in the wet grass, disappeared over the edge of the steep incline, beyond the swathe of vegetation next to the road. 'Stay here.'

Reece jogged over to the edge of the incline and Sara followed him, dropping to her knees and crawling to the edge. For a moment vertigo almost threw her forward and then she caught sight of the cyclist, focussing on him, and the world began to steady again.

'There he is.' She craned over as far as she dared to get a good look. 'He's not moving.' The cyclist was lying on a broad shelf about thirty feet down, seemingly unconscious. Edging another few inches forward, she saw blood in the area of his shoulder.

Reece's hand was on her shoulder, pulling her back. 'Take my phone and call the emergency services. I'll go and get the car.'

By the time Sara had made the call, and received a promise of a rescue team as soon as possible, Reece had backed the SUV as close to the edge of the incline as he could and had jumped out. He was rummaging in the back for something.

'Have you got anything to help us get down there?' Reece had cleared out the boot of his car yesterday, in order to fit in as many of Simon's possessions as possible, but it appeared that most of the things that had been removed had managed to migrate their way back again.

'Ah!' Reece had obviously found what he was looking for, and reached in, dragging a coil of rope from the boot. 'I thought I put this back in here again.' He coiled the rope carefully, checking it as he went, and looped one end of it around the towbar on the back of the car.

'I'll go.'

He froze. 'You will not.'

'This is my job.'

'Not in this country it's not. You're staying here.'

'No, Reece.' She pulled at his shoulder, turning him round to face her. 'Look at it rationally. If you go down there, I don't have the strength to pull you back up again. The safest thing for both of us is for you stay at the top and lower me down.'

He broke away from her roughly, striding over to the edge of the incline and looking down at the man below them. 'You're no good with heights, Sara.'

'That's when I'm on holiday. At work I've been on roofs, ledges, you name it. People don't just get injured on the ground, you know.' Sara knew that Reece would understand that. It was one thing not to choose to stare down a thirty-foot drop. It was quite another when there was a job to do.

He turned and walked back to the car. He was more pig-headed than she'd given him credit for. Then she heard him curse under his breath.

'All right, then.' He had pulled a climbing harness out of the car boot and he began to wrap it around her body and legs, pulling the straps tight. 'Do anything stupid and you won't need to worry about falling. I'll throw you over the edge myself.'

'Fair dues. Just concentrate on not dropping me.' The grim humour calmed her nerves.

He clipped the rope to her harness and checked everything thoroughly. In almost any other situation his hands on her body like this, treating it as if it were his and there was nowhere he couldn't touch, would have taken her breath away. Now it was just reassuring that he was being so thorough.

'Right. I'll have to lower you down the first ten feet, but then it's not so steep. See if you can get a handhold, and guide yourself down. When you get down there, don't take the harness off and keep your helmet on, whatever happens. You stay attached to the rope at all times, right?'

'Right.'

He rolled his eyes. 'I must be mad, letting you do this…' He got hold of the ropes that he had fixed firmly to the back of the car. 'Okay, off you go.'

## CHAPTER EIGHT

HE LOWERED her down, slow and steady, until Sara could get a handhold on the muddy incline, which was tangled with tree roots and branches. She scrambled down, and Reece played the rope out, ready to take the strain if she slipped.

'Okay. I'm down on flat ground now. Give me a few feet to work with and tie the rope off.' Reece's assent floated down and he disappeared for a moment.

'How is he?' His head and shoulders appeared again, straining to see.

'He's breathing.' Even though the light was fading quickly, Sara had already performed her initial checks. 'Seems to be coming round.' She bent over her patient. 'I'm a paramedic and I'm here to help you. Can you lie still for me?'

The man's eyelids fluttered in a gesture of assent, and Sara called up to Reece. 'I need a torch.' She could feel something sticky under her hands in the region of his shoulder.

'Coming down to you now.' She looked up and saw a large bag, suspended on a rope, being lowered towards her.

'Good. Got it.' She reached the bag and pulled the zipper. It was Reece's medical kit from the car, along with an assortment of other items. Reece couldn't be accused of having the tidiest car boot in the world, but he did have a lot of useful things in there. She grabbed the lantern torch and switched it on, setting it down next to the man.

'He's bleeding from a wound on his shoulder. I'm taking his jacket off for a better look.' Sara cut the Lycra cycling jacket and blood plumed out over her hands. 'I need something to pad the wound.'

She hoped that Reece would read the situation from that. Sara didn't want to shout that she had a bleeder on her hands while the man was conscious and might panic. The last thing she needed was for him to start thrashing around and tipping them both over the edge.

'Look in the bag.' He'd got the message. 'In a blue plastic wrapper.'

She snatched the packet out of the bag, tearing off the wrapper and packing the wadding against the wound. 'Okay, mate, this will hurt a bit, but try and stay still.' She applied pressure, and the bleeding began to slow.

With one hand she felt in the bag, searching for the things she needed, while she still kept up pressure on the wound. Reece was above her, and she could feel his gaze. Watching over her, and her patient, keeping them both safe.

He sent a blanket down and Sara wrapped it around the man. She kept him talking, telling him her name and finding out that he was a student, studying chemistry at Monash University. Together they crouched on the exposed ledge, as the minutes ticked by.

'I can see headlights.' Reece's voice again, floating down on the breeze. 'The rescue services will be here soon.'

'Hey, Patrick. Hear that? Looks like you and me are about to go up in the world.'

Patrick tried for a smile and failed, his eyelids fluttering down. 'Is it me, or is it freezing up here?'

It was cooler now that the sun had gone down, but Patrick had also lost a lot of blood and he was weak and in shock. Sara crouched over him, trying to shield him from the breeze with her own body. 'Is that better?'

'Yeah.' He managed the smile this time. 'Either I'm on death's doorstep or it's my lucky day.'

'It's your lucky day. Most of my patients get told to lie still and stop complaining, but I've taken a liking to you.'

'Right. So I'm not about to die or anything.' Patrick's ashen lips moved in a whisper.

'Nope. You've got a wound on your shoulder, but I've stopped the bleeding now and you're going to be fine.'

'Thanks. Don't suppose you can see my bike anywhere?' Now that Patrick's fears about his own mortality had been quelled, his thoughts were on his expensive racing bike.

'That's not in such good condition.' Sara could see the back wheel hanging from a tree root, and the rest of it must have gone over the side. 'Not quite as resilient as you are.'

'It's…insured…' Patrick's eyelids drooped downwards, and Sara looked desperately upwards, towards Reece.

'Not long now.' As he called down to her, his body was suddenly silhouetted against the glare of headlights. 'Just hang on there for another few minutes.'

She could hear Reece's voice and the sound of activity on the road above her. Sara crouched over Patrick, holding him tight.

Lights, the sound of motors and shouted instructions, and a carry cot came bumping down, followed by two men. They worked quickly, almost without a word, putting Patrick into the cot and winching him upwards to the waiting medics. Then, after what seemed like an interminable delay while activity at the roadside centred around Patrick, it was Sara's turn, and she half climbed, half let herself be pulled up to the top of the incline.

Reece was there. Steadying her when she stumbled to

her feet and guiding her away from the edge. Unclipping the rope, unbuckling her helmet and taking it off.

'Where is he?' Sara looked around wildly.

'Already gone. The ambulance guys wanted to get him to hospital as soon as they could.'

'Did they say…?' In the failing light, Sara had not been able to see Patrick's condition properly towards the end.

'He's in good hands. We can call the hospital to see how he's doing, but I checked him over quickly when he got to the top, and you stopped the bleeding in time. He'll be fine…'

Reece broke off, turning as someone called his name. 'Back in a minute.' His half-smile made the prospect seem delicious. Sara watched as he strode over to the mountain rescue team, who had finished loading their vehicle. A few exchanged words and he let them go.

'They've got another call. Gotta rush.' They were plunged into semi-darkness as the headlights of the rescue vehicle arced round, finding the road and tracing a path away from them.

'Bye, guys.' Sara intoned the words softly, giving a little wave at the receding headlights, and then turned to face him. Almost bumped into him, he was so close.

'Sara.'

'Yes?'

'Tell me you're not going to do this to me again.' He started to unbuckle the straps of her harness. This time there was nothing to divert her attention from the feeling of his hands against her body. Or maybe it was just that Reece seemed to be lingering over the task this time.

'Do what?'

He sighed. 'I've known you less than a week, and in that time I've had to collect you from the path of a bush fire and dangle you over the side of a mountain…'

'It was only thirty feet.'

'This is a mountain. It says so on the map.' He snapped open the buckle at her waist, letting the harness fall at their feet, and tucked one finger into the front of her jeans, pulling her towards him.

'Thought you didn't need a map.'

'Don't change the subject.' He curled his arms around her shoulders in a slow action that was nothing short of pure male possessiveness. Nothing could hurt her here, except perhaps the man who seemed to want so badly to protect her.

'I won't do it again. Unless…'

'Unless nothing. Or I'll take you home and lock you in your room.' His eyes were glistening in the half-light.

'Oh, yeah?'

'Think I wouldn't?'

'You might try.' He might be heavier than her and a great deal stronger, but there was no question who had the upper hand here. One move from her, one word, and he'd back off.

She reached towards him, her fingers brushing the front of his shirt, and the light in his eyes turned from humour to dead seriousness. 'I've already crossed this line once, Sara, and I've been thinking about it ever since.'

'Me too.' If he didn't kiss her now, she was going to have to kiss him. And she wanted more than anything for him to make the first move.

His lips touched hers, brushing them lightly. He tasted and then he took, and then came back for a second helping.

'I want more than this.' The finger that traced the line of her jaw told her exactly what he wanted. It was almost painful, that slow arc of desire, which burned through her with nowhere to go. Nothing to slake the heat that it produced.

'I…I want…' She wanted what she couldn't have. Long nights alone with Reece. Time to work through the attraction that flared between them, explore it, let it lead them wherever it was going to. Instead, she had less than two weeks, and that wasn't even close to being enough.

She could have listened to the voice of reason, but right now reason didn't seem to have much of a point to make. Reece was hers for the taking. All she had to do… She knew exactly what she had to do.

'No promises, Reece. I can't make any promises, you know that.'

'I know. Neither can I.' He chuckled quietly. 'Maybe just one.'

'Which one would that be?'

'Don't you know?' He backed her against the car, lifting her off her feet, his hands splayed around the seat of her jeans, supporting her weight. Tonight he was all hers, and he wouldn't disappoint her.

'I know. Kiss me again.'

'Thought you'd never ask.'

He kissed her as if all the hunger that had been building between them, all the uncertainties of the last few days could be set to rest by just this one kiss.

They couldn't, though, and she wanted more. Here by the roadside, on the damp grass, on the back seat of the car, she didn't care. She just wanted Reece. 'I don't suppose you have a condom in your car.' It seemed a reasonable enough request—he seemed to be able to produce almost everything else from the glove compartment, or under the seats, or from the capacious boot.

'Nope.' He didn't even pause for thought, and Sara suspected that even if he did, he wasn't about to use it here. 'Going to have to wait.' He kissed her again and all rational thought melted in the heat of his desire.

'Don't know if I can.'

'You can.' His hand found her breast, brushing it lightly

through her clothes. Closing around it, his mouth forming words of approval against hers as he explored its shape and feel. 'A short drive between the starter and the main course only makes you hungrier.'

It was *not* a short drive home, even though Reece was a lot heavier on the accelerator than normal. But driving with him in the darkness, the companionable silence hanging between them softened her hunger for him, turning it from a 'take me now or else' thing into something that suffused her mind as well as her body. Something that took its time, waiting, trembling at the thought of what might happen next, at the same time as revelling in it.

Reece skidded into the driveway and came to a halt. No time to park the SUV neatly alongside the house. No time for second thoughts but, then, Sara had none.

Reece hustled her into the house and switched on the hall light. He'd already pulled his shirt over his head, and his mud-caked boots had been left behind on the porch, next to Sara's. 'Let me see you, beautiful.'

'Hmm. You may have to catch me first.' She broke free of him, dancing backwards along the hallway, peeling off her sweater as she went and dropping it onto the floor.

'So it's like that, is it?'

'Yep…' Sara turned and darted away from him as he made a lunge in her direction. She sped into the kitchen and then doubled back when he blocked the entrance, ducking under the breakfast bar. By the time she had made the lounge and done a couple of turns around the sofa, they were both laughing. 'Slow, Reece. You're too slow.'

He vaulted over the sofa and grabbed her, in a cross between an embrace and a rugby tackle. 'Now who's slow? Ouch… No, honey, not the face.' Sara's arms were flailing, reaching for some kind of hold, and she had caught him square on the jaw with her elbow.

Before she could breathe, he had her on her down on the sofa, spread out beneath him, her arms pinned above her head. A grin curled his lips as slowly he started to unbutton her blouse with his free hand. She wriggled in his grasp, squealing with laughter, and he quieted her with kisses.

'You too.' She wanted him out of his clothes.

'Yeah?' He released her hands, pulling her blouse off. 'You've got a bit of catching up to do first.' One hand reached behind her back and before she knew it he'd got the catch on her bra undone.

'Hmm. Very impressive. Where did you learn to do that?' She slipped out of it, and his gasp of pleasure made her shiver.

'Sleight of hand. I can do magic, remember?' He was trailing his fingertips across the soft skin of her stomach.

'So you can.' Sara gave herself over to his caress. He wanted to see and touch and kiss then touch again. Gently he pulled off her muddy jeans and then gathered her up in his arms, to carry her through to the bathroom. He turned on the shower.

'Reece. Reece, wait.'

She pulled at the button of his jeans, snapping it open, and he grinned. Tugged the zipper and slid the fabric down over his hips, and he groaned at the touch of her fingers. Tonight that golden body was all hers.

He kept her under the shower just long enough to wash off the mud and sweat from the evening. Reece wanted to be clean for her, to do this properly, but he knew that they had to do it now. Even a moment lost was a moment that they'd never have again. He lifted her up, carrying her through to the bedroom, and she laughed with delight, wrapping her legs around his waist and kissing him so hard that he lost his balance and they crashed down onto the bed together, his arms only just breaking his fall in time so he didn't crush her.

'Now. Now.' Her body was urgent beneath his. Soft and giving, but insistent beyond all thought of resisting her. Trembling, he moved one hand down, between their bodies, to find out whether she really meant it and found that she did.

'Wait.' He would show her who was the stronger. He kissed her, nuzzling at her neck and breasts, and she cried out with frustration. Arched beneath him, her body was begging for his.

He'd reckoned on having the willpower to take it slowly, but he'd reckoned wrongly. When she cried out for him, he couldn't wait any longer. There was one short moment of stillness when he knew that this was the only place in the world that he was supposed to be, and then she choked out his name and pulled him with her into a place where thought and will had no say in the matter.

Reece tried to gather his thoughts, tried to give a name to what had just happened between them. It was no good. He kissed her flushed cheek and she nuzzled against him. The smell of her sweat was intoxicating. The feel of her skin. There was no name for this feeling. His body knew, but his mind had temporarily given up on him.

He folded her in his arms, feeling her heart beat against his chest. 'Sara…I'm sorry.'

'What?' She pulled back from him suddenly, and he thought he saw her eyes glisten with sudden tears. 'What for?'

'I meant to…' Dammit there was no way of putting this tactfully. No way that he could think of, anyway. 'I meant to go a little slower.'

'Oh. I thought you meant…' She dismissed whatever

she had thought as if it didn't matter, and grinned at him. 'Any slower and you would have killed me.' She wrapped her arms around his neck, kissing him. Her kiss told him everything, more than her words, and the warmth of sudden and complete happiness tore a chuckle from his throat.

'Maybe next time.'

'Next time?' Her fingers trailed across his skin, wandering playfully. 'There's going to be a next time, is there?'

'Sooner than you think if you keep doing that.'

## CHAPTER NINE

REECE had opened the sliding doors that led onto the veranda, and the warm night breeze had played over their bodies as they'd made love, slept and then made love again. As dawn broke, he lifted her onto his lap, face to face, supporting her back with one arm.

'Do you think we made that?' Light was slanting across the bed, turning his skin from russet to gold.

'The sunrise?' He thought for a moment. 'Why, do you think it'll stop if we do?'

'Maybe. Do you want to risk it?'

He shook his head, laughing. 'Don't think we should.' His fingers found the nape of her neck, caressing its curve. 'Did I mention that you have excellent postural alignment?' He nuzzled her neck, kissing it, while his fingers trailed down her spine. 'Very sexy.'

'No. Think you left that out.'

'Hmm. Remiss of me.' His hand swept the length of her back, cupping her head, and Sara shivered at the sensation. 'Little bit of tension. Just here.' He kissed her shoulder.

'Really?' Sara reckoned that every single muscle in her body had quivered with tension and then relaxed under his caress at some point during the night. If he'd missed one, it certainly hadn't been for want of trying.

'Yeah. Here, let me...' His fingers found the knots in her shoulders and started to work at them. 'How's that?'

'Little bit more. I don't think you've quite reduced me to jelly yet.'

He grinned. 'Give me a chance.' He dug his thumbs in, and Sara shuddered.

'Yeah. That's good.' She wrapped her arms around his neck. 'You have very talented hands.'

'My hands thank you. If there's anything they can do for you, they'd like you to feel free to ask.' He curled his arms around her, the warmth of his body making her shiver.

'Just that. I like that.' Kissing him was almost automatic. Her lips seemed to form in the shape of a kiss of their own accord, against whatever part of his skin was closest. 'What do you like?'

'Didn't I tell you?'

'Tell me again.'

He chuckled, lazily. 'I love to feel you come. It's like...' He nuzzled close, whispering in her ear.

Sara giggled. 'It is not.'

'It is. Can't think of another way to describe it. What, you don't like the idea of warm honey...?'

'Bit messy.'

'Uhuh. So beautiful and yet so practical.' His teeth nipped her ear wickedly. 'You want to let me feel that again?'

'There's no honey in the cupboard. I didn't know you liked it.'

'Ah. Literal as well. You're sweet enough...'

Words gave way to thought, and thought to action. Sara had not thought that she had any more to give, but somehow, from somewhere, it seemed that she did. His slow hands, those soft lips found a wellspring of feeling locked deep inside, and coaxed it gently to the surface.

He took his time. Advancing slowly and then retreating. Surrounding her with warmth and cutting off every retreat until there was nothing in her world but him. When he finally coaxed her body into surrendering to him, it was more complete than she could ever have imagined. Devastating in its intensity, demolishing everything and filling her up again with the sweetest sensations.

She turned her face from him. He mustn't see.

'Hey. Hey, what's this?' With astonishing alacrity, he seemed to snap out of the post-coital blur that had gripped him.

'Nothing. Nothing.'

'It's okay. Whatever it is…'

It wasn't okay at all. In Sara's experience the one thing most likely to make a man feel awkward was a woman's tears. And crying after sex definitely wasn't a good look. She rolled away from him, onto her side, screwing her eyes shut in an effort to stem the tears.

She felt him kiss her cheek. 'You could share it with me, you know.'

'Share what?' She twined her fingers with his, pulling them to her lips and kissing them in a desperate attempt to convince him that everything was all right.

'That I'm so damn good in bed that it brings tears to your eyes.'

She couldn't help laughing. It seemed that all her emotions had suddenly escaped from lockdown and were bubbling in her chest, ready to break free at the slightest thing. 'Perhaps that's it.'

'Ah. Knew it.' He pulled her close, and she turned towards him, snuggling into his chest. 'I'm not afraid of your tears, you know. You've been strong for so long now, you should give yourself a break and just let go for once.'

There actually wasn't much choice about it. Her chest

was heaving now, trying to gasp out the sobs, but they wouldn't come. Then the dam broke, and she cried. It seemed like the first time in years that she'd actually sobbed her heart out, and it probably was.

Whether by accident or design, he'd unerringly found the source of that throbbing ache, which seemed to follow her around wherever she went. 'I don't want to be strong, Reece. Just for one day, I want to be…' She couldn't say it. Just for one day, she wanted to be the one who was nurtured and cared for.

'Make it today.'

'I can't…' Gran still needed her. She couldn't just fall apart and forget that.

'Why not? You've got to put it down some time. Last night, I thought you were a strong, beautiful woman…'

'Guess I've disabused you of that notion, then.' She quirked her lips downwards. Red eyed and sobbing wasn't her best look.

'Yes, you have. You're a strong, beautiful woman, who has joy and passion and who wants to break free.'

She'd done that last night when she'd fallen apart in his arms. Sara wondered whether he knew it or not. 'Last night was… I loved it, Reece. Every minute of it.'

'Yeah. Me too. And I love it that you couldn't hide your tears from me.' He grinned at her. 'And today is officially your day off. You get to sleep late, and I'll make breakfast.'

He would take no arguments. And when he wrapped her in his arms, drawing the sheet over her, she couldn't think of any place she'd rather be. Or when she'd felt so relaxed. Serene almost. Like the calm after the storm. She began to float, and then drifted into a deep, dreamless sleep.

When she woke again it was almost lunchtime. The smell of fresh coffee and bacon drifted in from the kitchen, along with the sound of Reece whistling tunelessly.

She lay on her back, smiling. The sweet scent of their lovemaking was still on her body, and when she reached out she could still feel the warmth under her fingertips where he had lain beside her.

'What are you doing?' she shouted through to the kitchen. Sara didn't want to move just yet.

'None of your business.' His head popped around the doorway.

'Oh. Okay.' She shrugged lazily.

'That's the spirit. Just keep that up, and let me take care of you today.'

Warmth enveloped her, and she stretched languorously. 'So you're in charge, are you?'

'Yep. And don't forget it.' He ducked as Sara threw a pillow at him, and she heard his chuckle fading along the hall.

She'd demolished breakfast, and Reece had run her a bath. Sara added something from one of the bottles of toiletries that Kath had left and then slipped into the scented water. Twenty minutes later, after he had showered, dressed and washed up the breakfast things, she was still there, and he figured that must be a good sign. Up till now the only time she'd stayed still and relaxed for as much as twenty minutes had been when she'd been asleep.

'I called Simon.'

'Yeah?' She stretched lazily. 'Suppose we'd better get going.'

'No need. He's got some other people visiting this afternoon, and he suggested that you come in tomorrow.'

She pointed her finger at him, narrowing her eyes. 'No, he didn't.'

Reece shrugged. She was too quick for him, and he supposed he'd better just accept it. 'No. Actually, he didn't.

But he does have some other people going to see him this afternoon…'

'After you called them, no doubt.'

'After I called them, if you're going to split hairs, and Simon says that you're to take a break.'

'You told him I needed a break, did you?'

'No, I told him that you'd kept me up all night, leading me astray.'

'I led *you* astray!' She was laughing now, her grey eyes bright and full of zest for life. 'You were the one doing the leading, I'll have you know.'

He loved it that she seemed so free, so happy. And Reece allowed himself the delicious thought that it was, partly at least, his doing. 'Since you're so good at tagging along, how about getting out of that bath and coming to the beach with me?'

She was on her feet in a second, the water slopping over the rim of the bath and onto his shoes. 'The beach! I haven't been to the beach yet, and I've been wanting to go.'

'The beach it is, then.'

True to form, Reece didn't take her to just any old beach. He'd picked the exact one he wanted and drove for miles, past a selection of other beaches, before he reached a wide swathe of sand, turquoise ocean crashing onto the shore. They walked a little way, clambering over the rocks, until they reached a sheltered cove, where they could swim and soak up the sun.

They found a place to eat later then drove home. As the sun fell in the sky, he made love to her again, tenderly marking the end of this perfect day. One moment. One day that she could catch and keep, through all the others that lay ahead.

# CHAPTER TEN

'SO WHAT's on the itinerary tonight, then, sis?' Simon grinned at Sara.

'Tonight I'm staying in Melbourne and we're going for a meal.' Maybe she and Reece would stop off at the beach on the way home, as they'd done last night. Lie flat on their backs, hand in hand, watching the stars. She couldn't get enough of the stars here, so bright in the night sky.

'I guess I'll be breaking the party up when I get out of here in a couple of days, then.' Simon's steady eyes left Sara in no doubt that he was only half joking.

'What party?' Did that sound like a suitable response? Something that someone who had definitely not been partying every night for the last four days might say?

'You tell me.'

It was uncomfortable sometimes, having an older brother. Sara had forgotten all about that, but she was fast becoming reacquainted with the feeling. 'If you mean Reece and me...'

'I doubt that Trader's found himself a lady friend.'

The old anger tasted bitter. Sara tried the breathing thing, taught to her by one of her girlfriends, who had learned it from her relationship counsellor, and yet again it failed to work. 'Reece was a friend when I needed one.'

'Ouch.'

'I don't mean it like that, Simon.' Sara forgot the breathing and decided that honesty was the best policy. 'Just because you're my brother, you don't get to tell me what to do. Or vet my friends, for that matter.' She grinned at him. 'What you do get to do is to be there for me. Be happy for me when things work out, and pick up the pieces when it all goes south.'

'Pretty raw deal, if you ask me.' The brother that Sara remembered was still there. The one who knew her, and understood that she needed to draw the line somewhere.

'Yeah. Want the job?'

'I'll think about it.'

They were getting there. The realisation that they'd come a long way but still had a way to go felt much more healthy than glossing over things. 'Nothing's perfect, you know.'

Simon laughed. 'I thought you were, sis.'

'I might be the exception to that rule.'

'You just might.' Simon paused, running his finger idly up the side of the walking frame that stood next to his chair. Sara knew that motion.

'What? Spit it out.'

'I thought I didn't get to say…'

'You get to say. I just don't have to listen if I don't want to.'

'Right.' Simon rolled his eyes. 'You know Mum was difficult to live with at best.'

'I know.'

'And we both dealt with it differently.'

'Yeah. We did.'

'Then let me be the eldest for a minute here.' Simon's face—so like her own, according to all the nurses—became earnest. 'If a girl…woman…like you happened to get involved with a guy like Reece, you know what I'd say to him?'

'Hypothetically speaking?'

'Naturally. If this hypothetical couple happened to become hypothetically involved, then I'd tell him to watch out…'

Sara's eyebrows shot up. 'Him? Thanks for that thought.'

'Because my sister's a fabulous, intelligent, beautiful woman, but she draws lines around herself. She's done it ever since she was a kid. Mum never got to you the way she did to me because you had your own internal world where you kept yourself safe from her.'

'Have you been reading that stack of women's magazines in the patients' lounge again?' Okay, so she'd wanted honesty. Just not this kind.

'I'm serious, Sara.' There was a hurt look in his eyes.

'I know. I'm sorry. Mum didn't take you seriously, did she?'

'No, not particularly. But that's for another day. Today…' He shrugged. 'I'm taking Reece up on his offer to stay at his place for a while, just until I'm on my feet and I can drive again. I know I can't manage on my own at home at the moment.'

'And you just wanted to say?' Sara tipped her head towards his, in a remembrance of the way that he'd comforted her when she'd been little.

'I just wanted to say that Reece is a nice guy. If you like him, this is not the time to be falling for Mum's propaganda.'

If only it was that easy. The cold, hard truth suddenly reared up, slapping Sara in the face. She'd been forgetting about all of the tomorrows and just concentrating on her todays with Reece, but that couldn't last for ever. 'It's not that easy.'

'No?' Simon seemed disappointed. 'I thought you might say that. Any particular way that you can think of to make it easier?'

'Don't think so.'

'Right.' Simon seemed lost in thought. Maybe this was the time to tell him about Gran. Maybe not. She'd decided not to tell him just yet, and she shouldn't just blurt it out on the spur of the moment. She should think about it.

'Hey.' She leaned forward, taking Simon's hand. 'Thanks for looking out for me, big brother.'

She could see how much it meant to him. He'd not been her big brother for a long time now. 'Well, don't leave it all to me. Try looking out for yourself for once.'

In another life, maybe. Another time. 'I always do.'

Simon looked at her, narrowing his eyes. 'Sure you do. Whatever made me think otherwise?'

The search for some kind of suitable reply was abruptly halted as Reece appeared in the doorway. 'Not interrupting anything, am I?' He must have seen the look on Simon's face.

'No,' Sara got in before Simon could open his mouth. 'Where have you been?'

Out of the frying pan and into the fire. Sara didn't want either Simon or Reece to know that she'd noticed that Reece was late and that she'd been mentally counting the minutes for the last half an hour. Reece didn't seem to mind, and she kept her eyes on him, away from the *I told you so* look that Simon might be giving her.

'Just helping out with the preparations for the open day tomorrow at the surgery. Mary has a virus and I've managed to convince her that she's not well enough to be serving tea tomorrow, so we're trying to find someone else.'

'Sara can do it.' Simon had clearly not yet quite got the hang of when a brother ought to keep quiet.

'You'll be here, though, won't you?' At least Reece appeared to be offering her a choice in the matter.

'Not necessarily,' Simon cut in again. 'Maggie was going to come in over the weekend. I'll give her a call and tell her tomorrow afternoon would be good.'

'Maggie? I thought…' Reece tailed off abruptly. Obviously wondering whether Simon's on-off girlfriend had featured in Sara's conversations with her brother yet.

'You said that it was all over between you and Maggie.' Sara turned on her brother.

'Yeah, that's what I thought too. Apparently not.' Simon made a lunge for the table beside his hospital bed, wincing as he did so, and his phone clattered to the floor.

Sara picked it up and handed it to him. 'You could have just asked for it.'

'Spoils all the fun. Anyway, the physio said that I needed to establish my limits in the short term.'

'Yeah, that means doing what you can do, not what you want to do. There's a difference.' Reece glared at Simon.

'She said I should sit up for a few hours each day. And she works me pretty hard when she comes to see me…'

'That's because it's her job and she knows what she's doing.' Reece's eyes softened. 'Your job is to do as you're told.'

In the limited time that she'd seen the two of them together, Sara had already noticed an element of the big brother in Reece's relationship with Simon. To an outsider, Simon seemed the more settled of the two, with a house and a thriving architectural practice. But it was Reece who stepped in and called the shots when the going got tough.

Simon capitulated with a shrug and a grin. Maybe, one day, she'd have that kind of relationship with her brother. Until then they'd just fight things out between them, each trying to go their own way.

Simon was dialling, a smile on his face, and Reece rolled his eyes. 'I can't keep up with those two.' The words, sotto voce, were almost whispered in her ear, while Simon talked animatedly on the phone.

'Is she…?' She hated having to ask, and suddenly resented Reece for knowing Maggie when she didn't.

'Maggie's great. You'd like her. I'll get her to come over as soon as Simon gets home, and we can all have a meal together.'

'Thanks. I'd like that.'

Reece nodded and caught Simon's attention. 'Give Maggie my love. Tell her that she's to come over next week, before Sara goes back home.'

'Sure.' Simon spoke into the phone. 'You heard that?' He nodded, listening to the voice on the other end of the line. 'She says what about Tuesday?'

'That's good for me. I'm away on Monday night, with the travelling clinic, but I'll be back by Tuesday afternoon.' Reece looked at Sara and she nodded. He'd seen the problem and fixed it straight away. No messing around or arguments, and everyone seemed to be happy.

'Right.' Simon said goodbye, promising to call later, and laid the phone on his lap. 'So Maggie's coming over tomorrow afternoon, and Reece has his tea lady.' He gave Sara a wink.

'Hardly.' Reece shook his head. 'If you want to come along tomorrow, I could do with a bit of help with my first-aid demos. We can get someone else to make the tea.'

'Are you sure? I don't mind making tea.' From what Reece had said, the day was designed to combine some basic health education with family activities, and it sounded as if it was going to be fun. Sara had been thinking about popping in before going to see Simon in the afternoon.

'Someone will step up for that. I can use your qualifications elsewhere.' He winked at her.

'That's settled, then.' Now that Simon had got an outcome that he was happy with, he seemed to be tiring. 'So where are you going to eat, then? Sara's all dressed up for somewhere nice, so I hope you're not going to take her for a burger, mate.' Simon ignored the look that Sara flashed at him.

'Chinatown to eat, and then I thought we could go for a walk.' Reece grinned. 'Show Sara some more of the city by night.'

'Sounds great.' Simon picked up the nurse's call button pointedly. 'Think I'll get back to bed and watch a bit of TV. I'll call someone to help me.'

'You do that.' Reece made for the door, shaking his head.

By the time Sara arrived at the surgery, the open day was in full swing. Reece had got up so early that she'd hardly registered his going, and she'd busied herself around the house for a while, before taking Trader for a long jog. After hesitating over what to wear, she had settled for a pair of loose linen trousers and a pretty white top, which looked vaguely professional without being out of place on a casual fun day.

There was plenty of room for a marquee, which had been erected beside the main building, and several other smaller canopies, which shaded the refreshments table staffed by a horde of very capable-looking women and the children's face painting stand. The sun was out, and it seemed that half the population of the surrounding area had turned up, attracted by the prospect of supervised games for the children and a sociable afternoon for adults.

Sara made for the marquee and slipped inside. Working her way past the clusters of people, responding awkwardly as total strangers smiled and said hello, she caught sight of Reece.

He had obviously not worried too much about looking professional. Even in the unlikely get-up of a top hat and a bright waistcoat, he looked deliciously handsome, like a travelling showman who had just happened on the gathering and decided to join in. He was working the crowd like a professional, and Sara saw him bend and produce what looked like a chocolate coin from the ear of a solemn youngster.

'Hey!' He'd caught sight of her, and was trying to extricate himself from the group of children that had formed around him, but they wouldn't let him go.

'Reece.' Sara made her way towards him. 'What are you doing?'

It was pretty obvious what he was doing. None of the children gathered around him were likely to be afraid of going to the doctor any time soon.

'Mr Marvo, if you don't mind.' His eyes were shining and he was grinning broadly.

'I thought you were meant to be doing first-aid demonstrations.' Sara smiled back at him across the heads of the children.

'That's later. I get to transform magically into Dr Fletcher at about three o'clock. In the meantime…' He reached into a cardboard box behind him, which had been painted black and covered in silver stars, and pulled out a brightly coloured scarf, which he draped around her shoulders, and a flat black disc. With a quick flick of his wrist, it became a second top hat, which he offered theatrically to Sara. 'Would you do me the honour of being my assistant?'

The children chorused a 'Yes!' and Sara gave in.

'Just as long as you're not going to saw me in half.'

Reece chuckled. 'Nah. Although it's a thought. I could

stitch you back together later on as part of my first-aid demo.' He put the hat on her head, adjusting it slightly to what felt like a jaunty angle.

'Is she Mrs Marvo?' the solemn child piped up.

Reece hesitated for a moment, and then his mouth curved in a smile that wasn't all for the children. 'Yep. Now, let's see if we can find a magic wand, shall we?'

# CHAPTER ELEVEN

HE'D sprinkled stars, produced a whole truckload of chocolate coins, which had been eaten just as quickly as they had appeared, and made sure that he'd greeted and talked to every family who arrived in the tent. His hat now resided on the head of a three-year-old boy, who had fallen over and then forgotten his tears as Reece had picked him up and produced yet another coin from nowhere.

'What do you think?' For a moment he was free of the demands of the children and he gave that moment to Sara.

'It's great. Everyone seems to be having a good time.' They were strolling together around the open space behind the marquee, which had been set aside for organised games for the children, in the hope that they would let off a little steam before the first-aid demonstrations.

He nodded. 'Yeah. The practice manager organises this every year. We're a part of a community here, and those ties are very important to the practice.'

'Not to you, though?' Reece had already talked about his plans for the future, and even though they seemed to change on an almost daily basis, the one consistent thread was that he would be moving on some time soon.

'Yeah, they're important to me.' He shrugged. 'Everywhere has its communities.'

She shouldn't care about this. She would be leaving

soon. She was the one who was moving on, not him. Somehow it would have made it easier to leave and wish him well if she had somewhere she could visualise him when she got back home.

'Don't you ever feel that you want to settle down, though? Be with people you've known all your life?'

'I haven't known anyone my whole life. Apart from Kath.' He jogged a couple of steps to retrieve a ball that had whizzed in their direction and lobbed it back towards the boy who was chasing it.

He made friends easily, fitted in so seamlessly everywhere, that it seemed as if he'd been there for ever. But Reece's real loyalty was reserved for a very select few. Kath. The brother he'd lost. Maybe Simon and a few others. Sara didn't want to think about which category she fitted into. It didn't matter, anyway.

'Your father—where is he?'

'Doing the rounds in Western Australia. Got married again last year.' Reece shrugged. 'His fourth wife.'

Sara didn't quite know how to react to that. Her mother had scarcely even allowed a man into the house after her father had left, let alone approved of one, so she'd never had the opportunity to find out how she would feel about having a stepfather. 'Did you go to the wedding?'

He grinned. 'Of course. Kath and I flew up there for the week. It was a good time.' He gave her a quizzical look. 'My dad's a law unto himself. He's a nice guy and he was a great dad when he was around, but he's never going to be the one who's there for either Kath or me. We've both learned to accept that.'

Perhaps that's what she should do with Simon. 'Do you think…Simon…?'

'No.' He rounded on her with an intensity that almost made her jump. 'Simon's not like that at all. You and he have been through a difficult time, and he's not always been able to be there for you, but in his heart that's what he wants.'

'You know that?'

'I know it. Don't ever doubt it, Sara. You both just need a bit of time to learn to trust each other again.'

He seemed so sure. Almost committed to it, as if it was a cause that he needed to fight for, right there along with her. She trusted Reece's judgement and he was no liar.

'Hmm. I guess I wouldn't be here if I didn't believe you.'

'Guess you wouldn't.' He leaned over, his lips close to her ear. 'I'm glad you are, though. As assistants go, you're by far the most beautiful I've ever seen.'

Sara dug her finger surreptitiously into his ribs. 'Watch it, Marvo. I've heard all about you magicians. All that sleight of hand doesn't fool me.'

'Not what you said last night.' He was so close. She could smell his scent, almost feel his hands on her body. Suddenly she was engulfed in the pure, sweet sensation of just wanting him. 'You know that top hat really suits you. I could…' He left the thought unspoken, trailing his finger down her spine.

'Don't.' Her knees were beginning to wobble, and she didn't want to have to cling to him for support, not in front of all these people. Maybe Simon was right. Maybe she did put people in boxes. If that was so, then Reece was in a dark, velvet-lined box, which emitted sunshine every time she opened it. 'Not until later, anyway.'

He grinned. 'Is that a promise?'

She could make that promise. For tonight, at least. 'Yes. It's a promise.'

She was still trembling when Reece seated her beside him and started the first-aid demonstration. Thankfully, he was the one who knew most about suncreams, sunburn and sunstroke, and the first ten minutes required no input from her. By the time he'd moved from bites and stings to cuts, she was feeling a little more in control of herself, and she demonstrated the pressure required to stem bleeding, almost indifferent to his touch.

Their audience watched politely, but question time revealed that there was an appetite for something more dramatic. Broken bones, choking, heart attacks and drug overdoses, and then the fifty-thousand-dollar question.

'What if someone's not breathing?'

Reece called a halt. 'Okay, all of these things are serious medical conditions, and the first thing you need to do is to call for help. Calling the emergency services is the most important thing you can do and the best way to help anyone who's in any of those situations.'

'But isn't there something that you can do in the meantime?' A woman with a young child on her lap spoke up.

'Yes, there is. And a first-aid course with a registered provider will teach you exactly what you should do.' He picked up a clipboard from the table next to him. 'You can sign up for a course here. If everyone in this community attends a course then it's not a matter of *if* someone saves a life, it's *when*.'

A buzz ran around the audience, and Reece took the opportunity of passing the clipboard and a pen to someone in the front row. It began to circulate, gathering names as it went.

'What do these courses cover?' A question from the back.

Reece held up a pile of leaflets. 'It's all on here. Some guidance on simple first aid and details of what the course will teach you.' A grin spread across his face. 'And since we have a paramedic here, I guess that she can show you some of the basic steps better than I can.'

A couple of children in the front row began to clap, and Sara shot Reece a withering look, which he ignored. 'For the purposes of this demonstration, I'm going to be the victim…' he paused theatrically to make the most of the laughter '…I mean, the patient.' Before Sara could protest he was on the floor at her feet.

She glared down at him, folding her arms, and Reece propped himself up on one elbow, addressing the audience. 'Now, the first thing to do is to get help. Call for an ambulance, and when medical personnel arrive, you should let them take over.'

The temptation to let him just lie there and see how long he could hold his breath was almost overwhelming. On the other hand, 30 people were waiting to see what she was going to do next. 'Right, well, obviously, if the patient's talking then he's probably breathing.' She got on her knees, and pushed him back down onto the floor.

A shimmer of laughter ran around the audience. That was okay. If they laughed about it, they'd remember it. If they remembered it, someone might be in the position to save a life one day. 'Follow the instructions on the leaflet.' Sara went through each of the numbered points in turn, rolling Reece into the recovery position and pretending to clear his mouth.

'Now, if the patient still isn't breathing you can try this simple technique. Lace your fingers together like this…' Sara held her hands up for everyone to see '…and apply pressure here.' She laid her hands on Reece's chest.

'Not too high, or you'll crush the windpipe. Right on the…' Reece fell silent, gasping as Sara pushed hard, expelling all the air from his lungs.

'You see what that does?'

'Think I'll try that on my husband.' A voice came from the back of the group and everyone laughed.

'Yeah, it's useful for that too.' Sara grinned. 'Now, let's go through the checklist again…'

Reece woke the next morning, completely satisfied. The open day had gone well, Sara had obviously enjoyed herself and she was in his arms, still fast asleep. Last night he'd learned that sleeping with a woman wasn't just a euphemism for making love. Sleeping with someone had a whole wealth of meaning all on its own.

They'd got home late, both exhausted from clearing up after the surgery had finally closed its doors to visitors for the day. They'd stripped off their clothes and fallen into bed. He'd curled his body around hers, pulling her close, no hesitation in touching, even if it wasn't for sex. And they'd stayed close all night, as if that was the way that they were meant to be, and everything was all right with the world.

'Hey, you.'

'Hmm?' She shifted slightly in his arms, still half-asleep.

'Are you awake?'

'No.' She pulled his arm around her, cradling his hand in hers against her belly. 'Still dreaming.'

Longing gripped him, squeezing so hard that he almost cried out. He wanted in on those dreams of hers. Wanted to be a part of her, waking and sleeping. His fingers slid downwards, his whole body tense now, gauging her reaction. One sign from her and he'd stop.

She sighed and he felt her body relax against his. Almost melting into him, as if it were possible for the liquid sunlight spilling into the room to somehow fuse them together in its touch.

His other hand cupped her breast and she stretched in his arms, like a cat luxuriating in the heat of the sun. 'That's nice.'

Her speech was still slurred from sleep and she seemed

to be making no effort to come to. The realisation hit Reece that she didn't want to wake up just yet. Did she really trust him that much?

'Shh, sweetheart.' He dropped a kiss on her neck. 'You don't need to do anything. Just let me touch you.'

Her soft, sleepy laugh seemed to be laced with the music of bells. 'Hmm. Don't stop, then.'

Reece felt something prick at the side of his eyes. Not tears. Surely not. He dismissed the thought and concentrated on the matter in hand. He knew the caresses that would send pleasure rolling through her, the ones that would make her sigh, and those that would make her scream. She'd already given herself to him, trusting him to do this right, and all he wanted to do was to show her that she hadn't been mistaken.

Slowly, gently, he made his move. Waited until each breath was a sigh and then took the pace up a notch. She squeezed her eyes shut, fingers reaching for something to grip tight and latching onto the sheet that still covered them.

It was all for her. Her submission had turned him into her slave and everything he did was for her pleasure. Watching for each twitch of the muscle at the side of her face. Listening for each sigh, gauging whether it was deeper than the last.

Rolling her over onto her back, he pulled the sheet away from her. Tasted her sweat. Felt her shiver as his breath cooled and then reheated her skin. Found that the scent of her arousal seemed to change, grow sweeter, the further he pushed her.

'Reece.' Her hands were fluttering across his back now. 'Reece, please.'

'Do you trust me?' He wanted to hear her say it, more than anything in the world, apart from one thing. They'd promised not to talk about love, and he wouldn't break that vow now.

'I trust you.' Her words sent him spinning, light-headed, into a new world of desire.

'Then let me make love to you.'

'Please...yes...'

Reece had always reckoned himself a considerate lover, but this was something different. This complete detachment from his own pleasure, his only thought being for hers. 'I can't breathe without you, Sara.'

'You don't have to.' She seemed to know that she had broken his will completely. 'Make love to me and I'll breathe for both of us.'

He had a true heart, and a free and giving spirit. Sara didn't just trust him, she loved him as well. But that wasn't any part of the bargain. Love meant promises and there was only one promise that she could make to Reece. When the time came she would let him go. Not try to drag him into her life, her responsibilities.

They lay on their backs, watching the line of sunlight move across the ceiling.

'Probably about time for breakfast.' Sara had discovered that this was the perfect way to start any day. Waking up with Reece. Feeling him touch her. Showering together and then making breakfast.

'Yeah.' He rolled over, propping himself on his elbows. 'I love sex in the morning.'

She dug her fingers into his ribs. 'I noticed.'

He seemed to be weighing something up. 'And in the evening.'

'Noticed that too. How are you with lunchtime?'

'Lunchtime? Haven't tried that yet.'

Sara grinned. She'd bet that he had, but it was nice to

think that he was suspending judgement until they'd done that together. 'Only about four hours to go.'

He grinned. 'Yeah. I could take you down to the beach, swim a little, and we could give it a go.'

'Oh, and we can find a deserted beach on a Sunday in the middle of summer?'

'Good point. I'll take you up into the mountains, then. Or out into the desert and build a shelter for you. Wait until the sun hits the top of the sky and then drag you into my lair.'

'And you'll do all this by noon, will you?'

He laughed. 'Another day, maybe.'

There weren't many more days left. Simon was going to be out of hospital tomorrow. And she was going home next weekend. Somehow when Sara had been able to tell herself that there was more than a week to go, it had seemed like for ever. This time next week she'd be on a plane, on her way home.

There were days, though. Today and then five whole days. 'Okay. What do you say we go to the beach anyway? Can we find one where we're allowed to let Trader off the lead?'

'Yeah, sure. Let's do that.'

Reece had been wondering about the best time to ask. About how to ask. Whether to mention it casually over a meal some time, as if the idea had just occurred to him and he hadn't been obsessing over it for days now, or whether to get her somewhere quiet, where they could discuss things properly.

The morning's lovemaking had been more than special, it had been somehow transforming. And if he still couldn't bring himself to contemplate the idea of knowing exactly where he'd be in a year's time, he couldn't contemplate knowing for sure that he and Sara would be apart either.

It was going to have to be the beach. They'd walked for miles and he'd chosen a secluded spot, where Trader could run free. Reece had spent half an hour spinning a ball as far as he could throw it, and then Trader had decided that was enough and had lain down at Sara's feet.

'There's something I wanted to ask you.'

'Yeah? Ask away.' She was watching the ocean, following each wave as it crashed against the shore then ran up the sand towards her.

'Would you...?' He chickened out. 'Do you like it here?'

'You know I do.' She turned to him, her short hair blowing in the breeze, her face tanned now from the sun. 'What's all this about?'

He had her attention now, and there was no going back. 'I thought that if you wanted to stay a little longer...until Simon's better maybe...then you could both stay on at my place, there's plenty of room.'

The light suddenly went out of her eyes. He'd messed this up. He should have told her straight away that *he* wanted her to stay. In Reece's experience, if you asked the wrong question then you seldom got the answer you wanted.

'I can't, Reece. I have to go home.' Her gaze fell from his face, dropping to her feet, where Trader lay, and he looked up at her, sensing that maybe he was the subject of the conversation.

Reece took a deep breath to steady his nerves. 'Sara, I want you to stay. I think...' This wasn't working either. 'You're the best thing that's happened to me in a long time, and I know that you feel it too. I want us both to have the chance to find out where that might lead.'

When she looked at him again, her eyes were full of tears. Reece hated seeing her cry, but maybe this time... Maybe this time it meant yes.

'We said no promises.'

'Right. And I'm not asking you to make any promises now. Just to maybe stay around a little longer. Take one day at a time.' One day at a time was the sum total of everything he knew how to give. And he'd give it willingly to her.

'I can't. I would if I could, but…' She trailed off, staring at the ocean.

Maybe he should have done this somewhere else. Somewhere where Trader and the broad horizon didn't have such a call on her attention. Reece caught her by the shoulders, twisting her around to make her face him. 'Sara…'

She faced him, her lips trembling. 'No. I can't. You don't understand.'

She was right about that, at least. The urge to promise her everything just to make her stay battled with the sure knowledge that he couldn't keep such a promise. 'Explain it to me, then.' If she told him that she didn't care for him then he'd know she was lying.

She looked at him, lips pressed together, eyes blazing behind the tears. If he turned away now and left it at that, Reece was under no illusions that she would never mention it again. He didn't give up so easily.

'Look, it's okay to say no, but at least give me a reason. I'll tell you now that I'm not going to stop asking, not until you do.'

She scrambled to her feet, calling Trader to heel, and starting to walk back along the track to the car. Reece wondered whether he should just let her go, give them both a chance to cool off a bit, and then got to his feet. Cooling off wasn't going to help. Nothing was going to make any difference, not until he got an answer.

Sara had known this was coming ever since this morning. How could he not have asked? And how could she have denied that being with him was the thing that she most wanted in the world?

'You could at least tell me what I've done wrong.' His voice hissed in her ear.

Typical! 'Stop it, Reece. Why does it have to be about you all the time? Can't you see any further than that?' Sara froze, stopping so suddenly that he almost bumped into her. Her mother's words had flown from her mouth before she'd had a chance to bite them back.

'I'm trying to. You're not giving me much help, though.'

'No… No, I'm sorry.' She made to start walking again but he caught her arm.

'So tell me. Is it that you don't care for me?' The look on his face told her that he didn't think that for a second, he was just goading her until she gave him an answer. He held her in his gaze for long moments while Trader circled patiently, waiting for them to finish and start moving again.

'Say it, Sara. All you have to do is say it, and I'll forget about this right now.'

She couldn't. Wouldn't.

'Say it.' His voice was gentler now. He knew. There was no point in saying it now, he'd never believe her.

'No. You can't make me say that.' Sara grabbed at the last remaining straw she had. 'No promises, Reece.'

'I made no promises to care for you, or to want you to stay. I didn't make any promises not to either. That's what it's like when you begin a relationship.'

'That's not what I meant.'

'I see that now. You'd already made a promise to leave.'

'Yes.'

'Who to?'

They'd been here before. Come round full circle and ended up with the same question. The one that Reece was always going to return to if she didn't tell him.

'I don't want you to tell Simon.'

A shadow fell over his face. 'I won't.'

He didn't need to promise. In any case, that word had already been used and misused enough between them, and Sara didn't want to mention it again.

'My gran. She's booked into a nursing home while I'm over here. The only way that she's getting out of there and back home is if I go back to London.'

'You look after your grandmother?' His face was grave. Concerned. It was okay, he didn't need to be. Sara didn't want his concern.

'Yes, she has a flat on the ground floor of my mother's house. She doesn't get about much these days. She's ninety.'

'And Simon doesn't know?'

He was just asking. Sara wondered why this felt like an interrogation and put it down to her own guilt. 'He never asked and I never said anything. He's had enough on his plate recently.'

'And you were afraid of what his reaction might be.'

Reece was good. Took the facts, wove motive around them and generally came up with the right answer. Sara wondered if he'd ever considered a career in intelligence. 'Yes, if you must know.' She started to walk. Somehow it was easier to do this when she wasn't rooted to the spot, staring up at his face. 'I made a decision that I'd stick with Gran and look after her, and I'm happy with that. I can't stay here.'

She didn't have Reece's gift for saying just exactly what she meant, but the message seemed to get through. He was walking beside her, thinking hard. Suddenly he seemed to come to a decision. 'I can't go with you, Sara. Not like that.'

'I know. I'd never ask you to.'

'Does this mean that we're done here?'

'Yeah. I guess it does.'

The walk back to the car was a blessing in disguise. Reece spun pretty much anything he could find along the way high into the air, keeping both Trader and himself busy and on the run. Sara took the time to compose herself, try to forget that she'd just refused what seemed like the offer of a lifetime.

It couldn't work. Tim had broken his promises to her and walked away unscathed, but that had been different. If Reece did that, it would destroy his integrity, and she couldn't take that away from him. She loved him too much to change him.

'Reece.' He'd managed to avoid any eye contact with her on the long walk back to the car, but it was best to deal with this now. Get it over with. 'I was thinking that I might spend some time back at Simon's place. Just a few days, to sort things out there for him.'

'I'd prefer it if you didn't.' He still couldn't quite meet her gaze. 'You know I have to go upcountry this week for a few days. I may need to extend the trip a little and Simon shouldn't be left alone at my place. Kath's back from holiday tomorrow and if there's anything you need…'

'There's nothing I need.' He was doing the decent thing. Or running away. Sara couldn't quite picture Reece running away from anything, but maybe she was deluding herself. Maybe her mother had been right about some things.

He opened the passenger door of the car for her, and she saw a flicker at the side of his face. Tension. Loss, maybe. A small curve of regret on his lips. Her mother had never met Reece, so how could she ever be right about him?

'It's the best thing all round. I'll leave this afternoon.'

'This afternoon? I thought you were going in the morning.' He'd said he would leave on Monday morning and be back on Tuesday evening, when he'd told her about the clinic that the doctors in the area staffed on a rotation basis.

'I have to start early. It would be a lot easier to drive up there this afternoon.'

He was leaving her. Sara wanted to cling to him, beg him to stay, but she didn't have a leg to stand on. How could she ask him to stay when she was going to be leaving for good next week, and she had just told him that this would be the end of things for them? 'Okay. Yeah, sounds sensible.'

'You'll be all right to pick up Simon tomorrow?'

'Of course. I said so.' She had to get into the car now, before she broke down. Before she promised him anything, in return for another few days, and then broke that promise and left anyway. 'It's okay, Reece.'

He closed the passenger door behind her then let Trader into the back of the car. Swung into the driver's seat, with that easy, restless grace of his. So free. It would be more than a crime to try and change Reece. He was fine just as he was. If she couldn't have him, that was her problem.

'It's not okay.' He paused before putting the key into the ignition, eyes far away, somewhere on the horizon. 'But it's the only thing to do.' His face showed one momentary flash of bitter regret and then he started the engine.

# CHAPTER TWELVE

HE'D been gone for three days. Sara had picked Simon up from the hospital and brought him back to Reece's house, letting him take the spare room while she slept on the sofa. Kath had called in, back from her week away. Maggie had come to dinner and Sara had cooked. It was all done in a kind of daze, as if she were living in a bag of cotton wool, able only to hear the voices around her as muffled, far-away sounds.

Then Reece called. Sara picked up her phone from Kath's kitchen counter, excusing herself with a smile, and slipping out into the darkness of the garden. 'Hello.'

'Hey. Where are you?'

'Simon and I are over at Kath's. Did you try the house?' Small talk. Anything, while she steadied herself in the wake of the giddy sensation of having everything suddenly snap into sharp focus.

'Yeah. I reckoned if you weren't there you'd be with Kath. Are you on your own?'

'Yes.' Sara sat down on the steps that led from the veranda to the garden, the darkness of the evening folding her into its warmth. Alone with Reece. Only this time he was just a far-away voice. She pressed the phone to her ear, straining to hear every word, every intonation. Each unspoken thing.

'How are you? Is there anything you need?'

'Fine. There's nothing I need.' If she closed her eyes and concentrated, that might almost be true. He could almost be here, sitting next to her.

'And Simon?'

'He's good too. Trying to do too much, of course, but he's mending well. Maggie came over last night.'

'Yeah?' Sara could hear the smile in his voice. 'Do you like her?'

'Yes, very much. Simon's planning to come to London for a visit later in the year, and she might come with him.'

'That's great.' The question hung in the air between them. 'So you…?'

'Yes. I told him about Gran. I reckoned in the end that he had a right to know, she's his grandmother too. It went better than I thought it would.'

'I imagine it did. So he's offered to help you?'

Sara smiled into the darkness. She'd missed talking things through with Reece. The way he seemed to know what was bugging her before she'd even said it. 'Yes. I turned down financial help, and said yes to the video conferencing. Gran's going to love being able to see and talk to him regularly.'

Reece's chuckle sounded down the phone. 'Sounds like a plan. I'm glad it's worked out so well.'

She had Reece to thank for that. He'd pushed her into getting things out into the open with Simon, and he'd been right to do so. It had been Reece's trust that had helped her to mend her broken family when her own had not been enough.

She could almost feel him breathing. Long moments of silence, like the ones when they held each other, but this time, instead of feeling that they could last for ever, they slid through her fingers like quicksilver.

'You're not coming back, are you?' She knew now what he had called her for. If he was coming back in the morning, he could have waited to hear all this, face to face.

'No. There are some things that need to be done here. Now is as good a time as any to do them.' At least he didn't make excuses and pretend that staying away was anything other than his decision.

'You should stay, then.' She'd already given him everything she could, a lot more than it was safe to risk, and there was nothing more left to be done.

'Yeah. I'll call Kath and Simon in the morning and let them know. Kath will keep an eye on Simon until I get back.'

'Thanks.' At least she didn't have to face Kath or Simon's questions about why Reece was staying away. He was trying to make this easy, but not even Reece could accomplish that. Some things were just the way they were and couldn't be changed.

'Sara, I—'

'Don't say it, Reece.' Whatever it was, she didn't want to know. 'We did what we did. Let's just let that speak for us.'

He heaved a sigh, but it was impossible to tell whether it was one of relief or regret. Probably a little of both, if her own feelings were anything to go by. Relief that he wasn't going to make this harder than it was. Regret that it had to be done in the first place. 'It speaks for me, Sara. Better than words ever could.'

Maybe he was going to make this more difficult than it needed to be after all. If he had begged, then she could have resisted him, but this silence, with the memories of his face torturing her, was worse than anything. 'Me too.'

'I'm going to hang up now.' His voice again on the phone. He seemed to know that she couldn't.

'Yes. Thank you.'

There was a short, cracked laugh on the other end of the line, which gave the lie to the joke. 'Anything for a lady.'

There was an abrupt click and the phone went dead. Sara strained to hear beyond the silence, and there was nothing. He really had hung up. She thumbed the button to cut the call from her end, and laid her mobile down on the decking beside her. Voices and laughter sounded behind her, in the house, and suddenly she was plunged into deeper darkness as someone switched the light off in kitchen.

Shadows pressed in around her, imprisoning her, like the sliding walls of the haunted house in the old horror film that she and Reece had watched together. This time there was nobody to hold her tight, though. No handsome adventurer to gather her up in his arms and save the day. She felt her back bend as the suffocating weight that she had almost grown used to not having to carry any more settled back onto her shoulders.

Reece craned over the glass-and-steel balcony at Tullamarine Airport. He could see Kath's head below him, bobbing amongst the crowd, alongside Sara's. He fixed his eyes on her dark hair, almost wishing that she would look up. Just so he could see her face, one more time.

There was no point in him being here. She couldn't stay, and he couldn't see himself learning how to put down the kind of roots that would allow him to go with her. All the same, he'd driven a long way to get here, and had raced through the airport, desperately searching for the boarding gate for the eleven o'clock flight to London. Then he'd frozen. There was only one thing left to say and that was goodbye. He couldn't bring himself to do that either.

The women hugged, and Kath started to speak. He knew what she was saying, it was what Kath always said when they parted.

*'We'll say goodbye and we won't look back.'* Kath's hand went to her chest. *'I'll hold you in my heart until I see you again.'*

Sara nodded and said something. Her own hand went to her heart, and Reece found himself mouthing the words. *'I'll hold you in my heart.'* He wouldn't see her again but he could deliver on the first part of the promise.

The women hugged again and, too quickly, Sara turned away. The downward slope of the wide walkway gradually swallowed her up, first her feet, then her body and finally that dark mop of hair. He kept his eyes fixed on the spot where she'd disappeared from view. Maybe she would sense his presence, turn and walk back again.

'What the bloody hell do you think you're doing, Reece?' He'd stared at the walkway for so long now that it seemed to have burnt its way into his retinas, and Kath's voice shattered his concentration.

'Hey. Looks as if I've just missed you.' It wasn't a matter of wondering whether he looked guilty or not, more like how guilty he looked. From the look on Kath's face, it was guilty as hell.

'Pull the other one. Have you driven down this morning?' Reece nodded and Kath frowned at him. 'So you drove all that way just to hide around a corner and not say goodbye. What's going on?'

Kath had a right to ask. She'd filled in for him, looking after Simon and Sara while he was away. The trouble was, Reece didn't have an answer. He wanted a few moments more to stare at the spot where he'd last seen Sara, fix it in his mind, but he knew he had to go now. He couldn't stand guard on this place all night, and Sara wasn't coming back. He turned and met Kath's questioning eyes.

'Was she all right? This morning?'

'She was fine. A bit teary at having to leave Simon, but

that was…' Kath broke off as light dawned. 'Reece. What did you do?'

Reece forced a smile. 'You want a blow-by-blow account?'

Light dawned on Kath's face. 'No. Too much detail.' Her gaze dropped to his hand, where he held his phone, his keys and the small, blue box. 'What's that?'

It didn't matter now. 'Here, take a look.' He handed her the box and Kath opened it.

'Reece! That's beautiful!' Kath looked around wildly and then started to tug at his arm. 'Go and give it to her. Quickly, the flight's not leaving for another half an hour. You could flash your doctor's badge and say there's a medical emergency and that she's forgotten her pills or something.'

The thought that Sara would be here, within reach, for thirty minutes more was almost too much for him to bear. 'No.' He laid his hand on her shoulder. 'No, Kath. It's too late, and it won't change anything. She has reasons for going, and they're good ones. I won't make things any more difficult for her.'

'But this is so pretty.' Kath took the gold chain out of the box, holding it up so the heart threaded on it dangled, sparkling in the overhead lights. 'Surely you want to give it to her?'

Not any more. He'd thought it was a good idea, a sign that he cared and that all the things he'd said to her hadn't been just hollow words, but as soon as he'd seen Sara here, he'd known that he had to let her go. He'd always travelled light, and he had to give her a chance to do the same. He shook his head, unable to find the words that made any sense of it. 'We said goodbye already.'

Kath's hand flew to her mouth. 'That night, at our house, when she took the phone outside…'

'Yeah.'

'She seemed...'

'How did she seem?' He was still hungry for every last little piece of information about Sara.

Kath shrugged. 'She was sitting outside on her own for almost an hour. In the end Simon went and brought her in. She was very quiet, I thought she was tired.' She grimaced, tipping the chain back into the box and closing it.

'Why don't you take that?'

'What?' Kath pushed the box back into his hand. 'Not on your life, Reece. It's not meant for me.'

'It's pretty. Shame for it to go to waste.'

She huffed at him. 'It went to waste when you decided to stand here watching Sara go instead of coming downstairs and giving it to her. If you don't want it then you can throw it in the Yarra.'

Maybe he would. Sara was gone now, and he couldn't imagine having any other use for the pretty, heart-shaped pendant. If Kath wouldn't take it off his hands then it would be better if it was never worn by anyone.

'Where's Simon? Do you have to get back for him?'

'No, he's at my place with Joe and the kids so there's no need to rush back.' Kath linked his arm with hers. 'Coffee. I'm buying.'

'Sounds ominous.'

'Don't worry, I'm not going to give you the third degree.' His sister laughed. 'Not unless you want me to.'

'There's nothing to say. Sara and I were together and now we're not.' It was much, much more than just that. But however hard Reece had thought about it, however many options he had gone through in his head, he'd still come back to the same conclusion. He couldn't follow her, knowing that she was tied to one place. He'd never been able to resist the lure of the open road before, so how could now be any different?

'And who decided that?'

'It was mutual.' Now that Reece thought about it, he wasn't sure who had decided. It had been an instinctive reaction on both their parts, something that neither he nor Sara could change. 'Thought you weren't going to give me the third degree?'

'It was a rhetorical question. I don't expect an answer.' Kath fished in her pocket and drew out a ten-dollar bill, holding it up in front of him. 'From the look on your face right now, I've got ten that says it's not as over as you think it is.'

'Put your money away. You'll lose.'

'Well, I'm not afraid to try… Hey!' Kath protested as he whipped the note out of her hand.

'Then don't be a sore loser. Sara and I are done. We won't be bumping into each other in the street and deciding to give things another try any time soon. It's over.' Reece said the words with as much finality as he could muster, and turned, scanning myriad airport signs to find one that pointed to a coffee shop. 'Suppose I get to buy now.'

'You suppose right. And I want a sandwich, I'm starving.' Kath was obviously bent on not leaving Reece any change from his win. If you could call it a win.

'Sure. Is this an end to it?'

'You've made up your mind?' Kath knew him well enough to know that if he had decided on something, he wouldn't go back on it.

'Yeah.'

She shrugged, twisting her mouth in an expression of regret. 'It's an end to it, then.'

## CHAPTER THIRTEEN

'HEY, Gran, it's only me!' Sara shouted at the top of her voice, so that her grandmother would hear her.

'Obviously. Who else makes all that noise?' Her grandmother's clear blue eyes regarded her from the chair by the window.

'Well, I wouldn't have to if you'd wear your hearing aids.' She unwound her scarf from her neck and took off her gloves. 'How was your day?'

'About twelve.'

Sara laughed. 'That many?'

'Sally loves her murder mysteries.'

'Oh, and you don't, of course.' Gran loved a good murder, particularly if it was solved by a woman over sixty. 'So the body count's twelve. Everyone brought to justice all right?'

'Of course. They always are. I wanted the one with the blue eyes to get away with it.'

Blue eyes. Reece. Sara swallowed down the now familiar feeling of loss and sat down, pulling her boots off. It had been a month now since she'd looked into those eyes. When was she going to pull herself together and find something else to daydream about?

'What about yours?'

'My day? Zero body count. That makes it a good day, Gran, in my line of work.'

Her grandmother nodded sagely. Small, white-haired and dressed neatly in a matching blue cardigan and skirt, with a bold printed blouse and a pretty necklace. Gran still liked to look nice. 'Well done, dear.'

Gran made it sound as if she had personally wrested everyone she'd been called to see from the jaws of death. Sara decided not to tell her that her last call had been to someone with a minor ear infection. 'So, have you eaten yet?'

Gran looked at her watch. 'Yes, I expect so. Sally left something for you in the fridge.'

'Oh, she's a star. I'll just go and see what I've got.'

Sara padded through to the kitchen and pulled the film from the dish that Sally had left. The woman was worth her weight in gold. Caring, sensible and a fan of murder mysteries. It cost almost as much as Sara earned in three shifts a week to have her look after Gran, but that wasn't the point. It gave Gran a change of scene and someone else to talk to, and Sara got to keep the job that she loved.

She put the dish of lasagne into the microwave, and popped her head around the door of the sitting room. 'Would you like a cup of tea?'

'No, I've been drinking tea all day.' Gran beckoned to her. 'Someone phoned.'

'Yeah? They didn't try and sell you anything, did they?'

'No. It was a man. He wanted to speak to you.'

'Did he? Who was it?' Sara wasn't holding out much hope of finding out. If Gran hadn't happened to be wearing her hearing aids, she wouldn't have been able to hear properly, and writing a message down wasn't so easy with arthritic hands. Whoever it had been would probably call back.

'He left a message.' Gran produced a piece of paper

from the table beside her and focussed on it. 'He wants to speak to you and he'll call back.'

'Oh, that's okay, then…' The microwave pinged and Sara turned.

'Simon's friend, from Australia.'

She spun round so quickly that she almost fell over. 'Who?'

'He's a doctor, you know. We had a very nice chat.'

'Yes, I know.' Reece had called her. It must be six in the morning in Australia. The flood of pure, perfidious joy that shot through her body, suddenly putting something to eat and a sit down right at the bottom of her list of priorities, turned to fear. She'd agreed with Reece that they'd make an end to it. No contact. He wouldn't have gone back on that unless it was something important.

'Did he say what it was about, Gran?'

'He wants to talk to you. I told him you'd be home at seven and he could pop round if he wanted.'

Right. Reece obviously wasn't going to be popping round, but perhaps he'd call back. 'Did he say anything about Simon?' The only reason that she could think of that Reece would be calling would be if something had happened to Simon.

'He said that Simon is fine. He made me write that down.' Gran handed the paper to Sara.

*Dr Reece Fletcher. Simon is fine. Popping round after seven.*

All written painstakingly in Gran's tiny writing. It must have taken for ever to shout the message down the phone to Gran and wait while she found some paper and wrote it down, and Sara wondered how much the call had cost him.

'Okay. Thanks, Gran. I guess I'll hear from him, then.'

'Is everything all right?'

'Yes, of course.' Sara managed a smile, and grabbed the phone from its cradle. 'I'll just go and get my supper. Did you want a cup of tea?'

'Yes, I think I would. Thank you, dear.'

'Right. I'll be back in a minute.'

Sara hit the kitchen, pacing. What did Reece want? Maybe she should call back. She shook her head. He'd said he'd call back and hopefully he'd make it soon. She wanted to hear his voice. She just wanted to hear his voice.

It was probably nothing. Sara flipped the kettle on, and put a teabag into Gran's china cup, spilling the hot water into the saucer as she poured it. The phone rang and she grabbed it.

She took a deep breath, trying to sound composed. 'Hello.'

*'This is an important message about personal injury compensation. If you have been...'*

There was no point in shouting at the voice on the end of the line, it was a recorded message. Sara cursed it under her breath, jabbing at the button to end the call.

Her heart was beating so fast that Sara wondered whether she might be about to faint. Planting her elbows on the worktop, she put her head in her hands. Deep breaths. That was better. Her hands were shaking as she tipped the hot water from the saucer and finished making the tea, but she was under control. Just about.

The doorbell rang. 'What now?' Sara muttered under her breath, deciding to let whoever it was wait. She had more important things on her mind. Tucking the phone into the pocket of her cardigan, she took the tea through to the lounge.

'Who's that at the door?'

'No idea. Probably someone selling something that we

don't want.' Sara supposed she'd better answer it. 'Back in a minute.'

She flipped the porch light on and put the chain on the door, opening it a few inches. The dark shadow that had been hovering halfway down the front path, obviously unsure of whether anyone was in or not, advanced into the pool of light and Sara jumped back, slamming the door closed.

'Sara?'

It was Reece's voice. That made sense, as it was him standing on the doorstep. 'Reece?'

'Yes. Are you all right?'

'Yes...of course... Just let me take the chain off the door.' Good. At least her wits hadn't completely deserted her and she had managed to come up with an excuse for shutting the door in his face. Other than the obvious. Disbelief and joy fought with panic and lost hands down.

Her trembling fingers fumbled over the chain and Sara took a deep breath. 'Seems to be stuck. Sorry, won't be a moment.' Another deep breath.

'That's okay. Take your time.' His voice was gentle. Like warm syrup, flowing over her nerve endings.

'Right. Got it.' She slid the door chain free, took another breath and opened the door.

'I'm sorry if I startled you. I spoke to your grandmother on the phone earlier and she said—'

'Yes. I know. I thought that she'd got it wrong and that you were going to call back.' Sara pushed the phone handset deeper into her pocket, until such time as she could unobtrusively get rid of it. Reece didn't need to know that she'd been carrying it around with her in case she missed his call.

'Is this a bad time?' He didn't move.

'No.' She swung the door wide, stepping back. 'Come in.'

*What on earth are you doing here?* would have been

a bit more to the point, but they could get to that one in a minute. Sara closed the door behind him. 'So...you're here.'

'Yes. I'm here.'

# CHAPTER FOURTEEN

SARA had clearly opted for observation, prior to diagnosis and action. She stood in the hallway, looking more beautiful than Reece remembered, pulling her thick, knitted jacket around her as if it was a shield. He had thought that seeing her again might bring him to his senses and make him realise that not even Sara could live up to the picture of her that he had been holding so tenderly in his imagination for the last month. That was obviously not going to work.

So much for Plan A. That was okay, he had a back-up. He also had a number of carefully thought-out opening lines at his disposal, but none of them seemed adequate for the moment. Maybe it was the sudden change in temperature from the doorstep to the hallway that was making his head swim.

'I'm here to see you, Sara. I'd like to talk to you.' It was neither witty nor heartwarming, and didn't bear the faintest resemblance to anything that he'd anticipated saying, but at least it was honest.

'It's a long way to come.'

She seemed just as much at a loss as he was and Reece reminded himself that she'd had no time to prepare for this. If the truth be told, neither had he. He simply hadn't anticipated that seeing her again would make him feel this way.

'That's how much I want to talk to you.' Damn. That

sounded like emotional blackmail. 'I was here anyway, and…'

She sensed the lie immediately. 'Yeah, yeah. And you just decided to drop by.'

'I should have phoned first.'

'You did.' She smiled and suddenly the sun came out. It had been four days since he'd seen the sun and he was already missing it. 'I just didn't get the message.'

He only had to reach out. The city that had greeted him had been cold, grey and claustrophobic and, despite his habitual optimism about new places, so far nothing had changed that initial reaction. And here, after a long, cheerless ride on the Underground, he'd found everything that he needed.

'It's good to see you, Sara. But I really just stopped by to let you know I was here. Maybe I can give you a call in the next couple of days.'

'No.' She caught his hand, and the heat of her fingers was almost painful after the freezing temperature outside. 'Stay for a while.'

'Thanks. I'd like that.'

He couldn't tell who reached for whom first. All Reece knew or cared about was that Sara was in his arms, and he could suddenly breathe again. This was the complete opposite of what he'd come here for but, then, staying away from her hadn't gone as planned either. Nothing had worked to slake the longing that had burned in his chest for what now seemed to have been the whole of his life.

It was more of a hug than an embrace, thick layers of clothing insulating them from each other. Just like friends who hadn't seen each other in a while. Somehow that was worse. The closer he was to her, the more he realised just exactly what he'd lost.

'Hey. It's okay.' He stroked her hair, making sure not

to let his finger stray to her cheek. It wasn't okay, but that was what he was here for. Somehow he had to find a way to lay the ghosts that swirled between them and give them both a chance to get on with their lives.

'If you can stay a while, we can talk after Gran goes to bed.'

'I've nothing else planned.' This was the plan now.

'Sara?' A thin, clear voice floated out into the hallway and she moved in his arms, twisting her head around.

'Just coming, Gran. I've got someone for you to meet,' Sara shouted back at the top of her voice, and warmth flooded through Reece. He would have waited outside until she was ready to talk to him, she hadn't needed to invite him in.

'Do what? If it's that doctor again, tell him to go away.'

She rolled her eyes, grinning up at him. 'It's okay, she doesn't mean you.' Reece let her go, and she hurried to the open doorway. 'It's not *your* doctor, it's a friend of Simon's that I met in Australia. The one who phoned, earlier.'

'Well, ask him in, then. What are you doing with him out there in the hall?'

'He's just taking his coat off.' She disappeared into the room, her voice softly conspiratorial now. 'Put your hearing aids in, Gran.'

Reece took his coat off quickly, hanging it on the post of the dark stairway, and she was back again, beckoning to him. 'Come in. Reece, this is my grandmother, Lily.'

Lily was dressed neatly, her silver hair carefully combed and styled. Reece knew how much work it took to achieve that, and he knew how much love it took to achieve the bright smile that she gave him when he was introduced. He'd seen it often enough in the women who gave him tea and reeled off a list of medications by heart when he visited his elderly patients.

He could see the fatigue that slowed Sara's movements from time to time as well. The way she leaned back in her easy chair, her gaze never leaving him, while he answered Lily's questions about Australia and his life there.

'You've come at a very good time.' Lily gave him an approving nod. 'I'm off on a little journey myself tomorrow, so Sara will have some time to show you around.'

Reece tried not to look at Sara and failed. She had reddened slightly, but she said nothing. The least contentious way forward seemed to be to concentrate on Lily's journey rather than Sara's free time. 'Where are you going?'

'I've decided to go back to the care home I stayed at when Sara was in Australia. It's a nice place and I'm well looked after there. And Sara will have some more time to herself during the week.' Lily's tone brooked no argument.

'This is still your home, Gran.' From the look on Sara's face Reece could see that she was not as comfortable with the idea as her grandmother was.

'Yes, and I'll be coming back every weekend.' Lily and Sara were obviously going over old ground here. Revisiting it again and again until they were both comfortable that the other was happy with it.

'Sounds like the best of both worlds.' Reece knew he shouldn't really be venturing an opinion on this, but he wondered whether Sara had spoken to anyone else about her obvious reservations.

'I hope so.' Her grey eyes were thoughtful, but she seemed pleased with his comment. As if she cared about his opinion. Suddenly it was important to him that she did care.

She seemed to relapse into her own thoughts, while Reece talked to Lily, only breaking in when it was obvious that her grandmother was beginning to tire. Lily bade him goodnight, and the two of them left Reece in the small sitting room.

'Right.' Sara breezed back in on a tide of warmth and energy, light years away from the slow, measured pace that she lived at when Lily was awake. 'Gran went out like a light when I put her to bed, so we can go upstairs.'

'If you want to stay down here, just to make sure she's settled…'

'No.' Sara grinned at him. 'I have technology for that.'

She led him into the hallway, catching up his coat and running up the stairs. The door at the top of the stairs opened into another world. A confection of architectural features that Simon would have been proud of, and which Sara didn't give a second look as she showed him into a large kitchen.

'Wow! This is…' He had imagined Sara in a range of different environments, but this hadn't been one of them. Downstairs, her grandmother's living quarters were a little old-fashioned but cosy and welcoming. This was sleek, beautifully designed and about as homely as a high-class office building.

'Yeah, I know. Not really me, is it?' She produced a pink gizmo of some kind from the kitchen drawer and flipped a switch on the bottom of it, holding it to her ear before she planted it in the middle of the shiny centre island.

'Baby alarm?'

She nodded. 'Gran's got a call button, but she doesn't always press it when she gets up in the night. This is my back-up surveillance system. Are you hungry?'

'I've eaten. Don't let me stop you, though.' He'd seen a plate of food in the kitchen downstairs, but she'd tipped it into the bin before he'd been able to enquire whether it was her dinner.

'I'm fine. I'll make coffee.'

She busied herself with an industrial-looking coffee-maker, and opened the freezer, pulling out part-cooked French bread and putting it into the oven. Suddenly the shiny, sterile kitchen started to look, and smell, like home.

'So.' She plumped herself down on one of the bar stools, next door but one to where he was sitting. 'What brings you here, Reece?'

She'd brought him. 'We didn't get to say goodbye.'

She nodded, suddenly solemn. 'No, we didn't. That doesn't mean we didn't both agree on the best course of action. I haven't changed my mind about that and I'm guessing that you haven't either.'

'That's not my point. We knew we had to finish it, but neither of us could bring ourselves to do it properly.' Whatever properly was. At the moment all that Reece knew was that they hadn't achieved it yet.

She shook her head in a sudden display of impatience. 'So you've flown ten thousand miles just to say goodbye to me, have you? Couldn't you have phoned?'

'No.' He laid his palms on the cool marble counter top in front of him. 'Can you honestly tell me that a phone call was enough the last time?' It hadn't been enough for him. It had left him a prisoner in his own home, bound to a house that he didn't even care about, just because she'd been there. The world had shrivelled around him, and there had been only one place to go if he wanted to find his freedom again.

She pressed her lips together tightly, jumping to her feet and marching across to tend to the coffee. Frothing the milk and banging the jug rather too hard on the counter top, so that she spilled some of it.

'Can you?' He was more sure of his ground now. He knew Sara. If she'd been that certain that parting was the best thing to do, she would have been kinder. If she screamed at him and threw things, he knew he was in with a chance.

'What? What do you want me to say, Reece?'

'Just give me an answer. Do you feel as if we really said goodbye?'

Sara wanted to shake him. Hard, until it knocked some sense into that thick head of his. She'd kept the emotion of seeing him again pretty much under control while she'd had Gran to concentrate on, but suddenly it reared up, smacking her in the face. 'We didn't need to... Oh!' Her gesture of frustration, anger, she didn't know what, had flipped the jug over and there was milk everywhere.

'No?' He jumped as she slammed the metal jug into the sink. 'Are you sure about that?'

Of course she wasn't. Sara grabbed a tea towel and dabbed ineffectually at her cardigan, then gave up and turned her attention to mopping up the spilt milk. She could almost feel his gaze on her back.

'I really don't know why you came here, Reece. There's nothing more to say.'

'Can you face me and tell me that?' His voice was closer now, right over her left shoulder, and Sara jumped. 'If you can face me and tell me that there's no unfinished business left between us, I'll go.'

She couldn't do that. Wouldn't do it. And he obviously wasn't listening to her silent agonised pleas for him to back off. He reached around her, and took the dishcloth from her hand, throwing it into the sink.

'Look, Reece, this isn't the time. I've got a lot on my plate right now...' She puffed out a breath and turned to face him. Tried not to look into his eyes. 'Tomorrow's going to be a busy day, and I'm truly not sure how I'm going to do everything that needs doing.'

Some of her anguish must have showed on her face because he stepped back. 'Is there anything I can help you with?'

'No. I can manage.'

'I don't doubt it. That doesn't mean that you're not allowed to accept some help.'

'It doesn't mean that I have to either.' Tears began to prick in her eyes. She didn't have to cry either. Whatever he did, and whatever he said, there was no rule written down anywhere that said she had to cry.

'And you're feeling guilty?'

Of course she was feeling guilty. Guilt went with the territory. 'It's the best thing for Gran. It's what she wants.' Sara took in a gulp of air. She knew exactly how this must look to Reece. She'd left him, telling him that she had no choice, and now he'd turned up to find that Gran was on her way to a care home. 'Things haven't changed, Reece. She still needs me.'

'I know that.'

'She's made me her legal guardian, and I need to be here to see to things for her. Make decisions for her if ever she can't make them herself. And there are the day-to-day things. Shopping, visiting…' Sara broke off. She was protesting too much and this was beginning to sound like an excuse.

'Hospital appointments, taking her out to see her friends. Giving her the reassurance of being there so that she knows she has choices.' He grinned. 'I know, Sara. I've never had to care for someone like this, but I know what it entails.'

'I just don't want you to think…' She didn't want Reece to think that she had lied to him. That it had been easy for her to walk away from him. 'I know how this looks.'

'It looks as if you let your gran do things in her own time. You helped her stay in her own home for as long as she wanted to, and now she's ready to go somewhere new.'

His eyes were darker that she remembered. Maybe a trick of the light. A deep, swirling blue that seemed to penetrate right into her thoughts, sifting through the hopes and fears that she kept so tightly under wraps. 'Thanks. For understanding.'

Reece turned away from her, one hand sweeping through his hair. That familiar tousled look that set the memories of sunlit mornings playing again in her head and almost made her choke with grief.

'I just wish I understood how to respond…' He sounded almost angry. Uncertainty wasn't Reece's style, and the emotion was obviously exasperating him.

She had no answers for him right now, and Sara knew that was dangerous ground. She needed a few minutes on her own, away from that magnetic pull of his that turned her thoughts upside down. A clatter sounded from the baby alarm and Sara silently thanked Gran for her good timing. 'Wait a minute. I'll be back.'

She spent a little more time downstairs than she strictly needed to, sitting by Gran's bed until she was asleep again. Tomorrow was going to be a tough day, both physically and mentally, and she would have given anything to have Reece with her. But it wasn't fair on either of them.

'We have to manage without him, eh, Gran? However hard it is.' She whispered the words so as not to wake her grandmother, tears rolling down her cheeks as she did so. This was no good. She had to go upstairs and face Reece, tell him the lie that she hadn't been able to tell him earlier. She crept silently into Gran's small kitchenette and splashed cold water onto her face, drying it carefully with a piece of kitchen towel.

She hadn't heard his footsteps on the stairs but the front door, clicking shut, made her jump. Sara's first instinct was to go after him, until she realised that Reece had done just exactly what she'd wanted him to do. He'd gone.

Upstairs, the kitchen was empty. The newly heated bread had been taken out of the oven and lay cooling on the hob. The baby alarm was in a slightly different place from usual. Sara picked it up and reddened when she found that it was still on. She could have sworn she'd switched it off before going downstairs.

There was one cup of coffee, by the bar stool where she'd sat, made just the way she liked it. A note, folded over in the saucer.

He'd written just two words, in the centre of the page. 'Until tomorrow.'

# CHAPTER FIFTEEN

SARA was a sitting duck, and she knew it. She couldn't rush Gran out of bed, or get her washed and dressed any faster, and once that was done, she needed to finish packing up the things that her grandmother wanted to take with her. All she had left to do now, though, was to load up the car, give Gran a cup of tea and then they could go.

She'd allowed herself to hope a little too soon. Just as she'd finished stacking everything in the hall, Gran picked up her extending grabber, catching the net curtain deftly between the pincers and pulling it to one side.

'Go and let Reece in, dear. He looks absolutely frozen out there.'

'Right. I dare say he's just popped in for a cup of tea.' Like hell he had. He looked cheerful and ready for action, and the mortifying thing about it was that, despite all her resolve of the previous night, Sara was actually glad to see him.

At least he had the grace to look a little sheepish when she opened the door. Didn't even attempt to come inside, even though she stood back from the door in an indication that he should.

'Can I move those for you?' He indicated the boxes and cases in the hall.

He was here, ready to work, to give her the support she

needed. She should just accept it. There was nobody she wanted more right now, and anyway she could no more turn him away than tap him with a wand and make him disappear.

'Thanks.' The one word constituted an agreement between them, and he nodded slowly. 'I'll bring my car around to the front door.' Sara picked up her car keys from the hall table.

'That's okay, I can do it…if you'd like me to.' He was carefully drawing the lines between them. Making the boundaries clear. Reece, the man whose second nature was to act rather than to ask, was deferring to her.

'That would be great. I was just about to make some tea for Gran.' She pointed across the street. 'That's mine, the red one.'

'Stick shift?' He grinned slowly.

'Yeah. Think you can manage it?'

'I'll do my best.' He took the keys, without even brushing her palm with his fingers, and another line was drawn. Jokes were okay. Even an exchanged smile. No contact, though.

The truce held. Gran left her home on his arm, guided safely to the car, while Sara followed behind at a discreet distance. Gran might be over ninety, but she still preferred a young man's arm to her ugly, grey walking frame.

'It looks like a nice place, Lily.' Reece walked Gran to the front door and left her with the job of pressing the bell. 'You'll have to show me around.'

'If you like.' Gran batted away the carer who came to greet her and started to make for the dining room, Reece supporting her all the way. 'Come and see in here, I think you'll find the view interesting.'

Being relegated to second fiddle, left to park the car

and get Gran's suitcases out, was nothing short of a delight. Reece was professing interest and approval for everything Gran showed him, and if he didn't notice the second glances that he got from women of all ages, Gran certainly did. For the moment she was the belle of this particular ball, and when you were ninety, you didn't let chances like that slip away easily.

'I'll call someone and get a cup of tea.' Reece and Gran had finally made it to Gran's room, where Sara was hanging her clothes in the wardrobe. 'Or would you prefer coffee, Reece?'

'Coffee would be great, if it's not too much trouble. Shall I call someone?'

'No, that's all right. I'll do it.' Gran was installed into her chair and was fiddling with the call button when a carer popped her head around the door, smiling.

'Everything all right?' The question was aimed at Gran, and Sara kept her mouth firmly shut. When she looked at Reece, he was doing the same.

'Yes, thank you. Only we'd like some tea, please. And a cup of coffee for Reece.'

'Sure.' The carer winked conspiratorially in Gran's direction. 'Make sure the workers have a break, eh, Lily? Get more out of them that way.'

'Quite.' Gran beamed back and Sara felt the muscles across her shoulders relax by one more notch. Every small kindness was like a balm spread over her fears for Gran.

'Right.' Reece picked up Sara's car keys from the bed, seemingly confident that she wouldn't object. 'I'll go and fetch the rest of the things from the car.'

He'd given Gran the instructions for the flat-pack chest of drawers and had spread the various bolts and screws out on the table next to her, so she could sort them into piles. Once that had been assembled, he'd taken the new TV out of its box, plugged it in and tuned it, while Sara had sat with Gran, drinking tea and admiring the clarity of the picture.

Then it was time to go. Sara knew that Gran would be fine. She knew this was the best thing for her. That didn't matter, it was still tough to leave her. Reece kissed Gran on the cheek and said goodbye, leaving Sara alone with her.

'It's time for you to go. I'll be all right here.' Gran stroked her cheek.

'I know. If I thought for one minute that you wouldn't then you'd be coming straight back home with me.' Sara didn't want to let go of Gran's hand. 'There's some flower arranging in the activities room this afternoon, if you fancy it.'

'I've got flowers.' Gran indicated the bunch that Sara had put on the windowsill. 'There are plenty of people here, I won't be lonely. Don't you be either.'

'Me? I'll be fine. Anyway, I'll be seeing you tomorrow, and we'll have the weekend together next weekend…'

'And in the meantime, you go and have a good time with Reece. Now give me a kiss, darling, and off you go.'

'Do you think she'll be all right?' Sara had done three months of research before she'd allowed Gran to come here while she herself was in Australia. Talked to people, visited different care homes, read reports. Gran had liked it, and had wanted to come back. But suddenly Reece's opinion seemed more important than all that.

'I think it's a great place.' He was leaning against her car, waiting for her. 'This isn't an end for Lily, you know.'

'Have you been talking to the manager here? That's exactly what she says.' Sara could feel herself beginning to relax.

'I did meet her while I was downstairs.' He grinned. 'Nice lady. She was telling me how she's working on strengthening links with the community here. Bringing people in so that the residents can still engage with different kinds of people, follow their own interests.'

'Yes. You didn't tell her that you do magic tricks, did you?'

'No. Why?'

'You'll be roped in for an afternoon's entertainment if you do.'

He chuckled, his eyes dancing. Ever since he'd been here, he'd seemed so controlled, so tightly reined in. Suddenly here was a glimpse of the free spirit she loved so much. 'Maybe I'll volunteer, then.' He pursed his lips, seeming to come to a decision. 'I'd offer to take you for a late lunch, but I've got two problems.'

'Yeah? I might refuse. What's the other problem?'

'First, I've no idea where to find a decent eatery around here and, second, you'll have to do the taking, because you've got the car keys.' He knew that there wasn't much chance of her refusal.

She dangled the keys in front of him. 'Does that make things any easier?'

He grinned. 'Yeah. One down, one to go.'

The problem, it seemed, was not with Reece's driving but with Sara's directions. She had meant to guide him past the underground station and then on to the multi-storey car park, so that they could walk to the high street and make their choice of where to eat. Instead, she'd got them stuck in a long tailback of traffic.

'Is it usually this bad?' He seemed to be taking it in his stride, but Sara was getting agitated.

'No, not at this time of day. There must be something going on up ahead, this lot's not moving.'

'Can we go another way?' He indicated a side road.

'No. That's just leads you into a one-way system that comes out on the other side of where we want to go.' She craned her neck, trying to see what was going on up ahead. Maybe an accident. Maybe she should go and see.

Reece was obviously thinking the same. 'Slide over, I'll go and see what I can see.' He got out of the car and Sara climbed across into the driver's seat.

'Anything?'

'Nothing that I can see. This jam seems to go right up to the next corner.' He jumped back into the passenger seat of the car. 'I don't hear anything—' He broke off as the unmistakeable sound of an emergency siren came from behind them.

The car was nosing through the traffic, switching lanes, using every inch of space to get past the stationary cars. Sara swung the steering-wheel, ready to turn out of its path, and was blocked by another car, inching its way along the inside lane.

Reece wound down the car window and leaned out. 'Can you move? We need to get out of the way, mate.'

The driver of the other car ignored him, inching forward still, taking advantage of a few feet of empty space in front of him to get just that little bit closer to wherever it was he was going. Reece gave a huff of impatience and was about to get out of the car when Sara stopped him.

'Leave it.' She manoeuvred the car so that she was almost touching the one in the next lane. 'They can get through there.'

'Can they?' Reece twisted round to check the oncoming vehicle's path.

'Yeah. Piece of cake.'

She turned and seemed to recognise the occupants of the emergency vehicle, flashing her headlights as it nosed past. Reece recognised the signal. I'm here. Ready to help if you need it.

It looked as if they did need it. Sara's mobile rang and

she pulled it from her bag, sliding it into the hands-free clip on the dashboard. 'What's up?'

'There's been a fire. Just around the corner in the high street. We'll know more when we get there, but there may be multiple casualties.' A man's voice crackled down the line.

'Okay, I'll see you there. Save a few for me.'

'Right you are.'

She glanced across at him, and Reece nodded. No need for words, there was no way that either of them would be continuing their journey to take a leisurely lunch now.

The lights changed up ahead and she switched on her hazard lights, changing lanes and cutting through the traffic to turn left. The junction up ahead seemed to be semi-organised chaos, vehicles trying to turn and being diverted on ahead by a couple of policemen, and Sara stopped at the tape that was stretched across the road.

'Paramedic. Let me through.'

One of the policemen nodded and waved her through, and Sara accelerated along the few hundred yards of empty road that led to a large department store. Reece could see fire trucks and an ambulance, along with other emergency vehicles. Great gusts of black smoke were issuing from the open mouth of the store.

They were both out of the car as soon as she cut the engine, and Reece followed Sara over to where one of the paramedics from the car that had passed them was unloading the vehicle.

'Jack. What's the story?'

Jack shook his head. 'We're not sure yet. Some kind of electrical fire probably, the whole street's shorted out. Two already on their way to hospital and we've got some minor cuts and burns, shock and smoke inhalation. There are an unknown number of people in there still, trapped in a lift between the basement and ground floor. The fire crews are working to get them out.' He seemed to notice Reece for the first time. 'Who's this?'

'He's a doctor.' Sara's voice was firm.

'Done any emergency work?' Jack's gaze was laden with suspicion.

'I'm in general practice at the moment, but I was a flying doctor in Australia for three years. Before that I worked in the emergency room in several different hospitals.'

Jack nodded. 'Okay.' He reached into the back seat of the SUV. 'Here.' He handed Sara a bright yellow jerkin with the word 'Paramedic' across the back. ''Fraid we haven't got anything that says "Doctor". You're the only one we've got here.'

'That's okay. I'll manage. Where do you want me?' Reece knew where he needed to be. The situation up here was under control and there was no one seriously injured. The stranded lift was an unknown quantity. This was Jack's operation, though, and he had no wish to challenge his authority.

Jack nodded, and a hint of a smile crossed his face. 'Inside with Sara, in case there's anyone injured in that lift.'

'Right you are.' Reece took the heavy medical bag that Jack proffered and started towards the entrance to the shop. Behind him he could feel Sara's presence and hear Jack's shouted instructions for the firefighters to let them through.

'Sorry about that.' Sara caught him up and was half running to match his stride. 'He shouldn't have—'

'He should. Jack's trying to deploy everyone where they can do the most good. He needs to know who's got what experience, and he doesn't have time for social chit-chat.'

She grinned at him. 'Yeah. Only Jack doesn't have much time for social chit-chat at the best of times.' She offered him the jerkin. 'Do you want to be the one with the badge?'

Her pace didn't slacken and she hardly looked at him, but he could see the side of her mouth twist.

'Nope. You're the fully paid-up member of the NHS, not me. I'm just an innocent bystander.' He grinned at her. 'You get to be the official help.' Despite the seriousness of the situation, Reece wanted to smile. They were a team again. Two people, acting as one. He felt almost light-headed with excitement.

She nodded and pulled the jerkin on over her thick, padded jacket as they followed one of the firemen through the blackened doors of the store.

'We've opened the lift doors at ground-floor level and the lift's stuck lower down.' Their guide briefed them as they walked. 'The emergency engineer got here in record time after we called, they're based just around the corner. He's checked out the shaft and the cables and there's a team downstairs now, working on the doors in the basement. Hopefully the lift car is far enough down that we can get whoever's in there out that way.'

Their feet clanged on the metal treads of the stationary escalator as they hurried down. 'The fire didn't reach the lift shaft, though?' Reece didn't want to think about what they might find in the lift car if it had.

'No. There'll be some smoke down there but hopefully not too much.'

The basement was in complete darkness, so they only had the light from their torches to guide them. Smoke hung in the air, and Sara felt her eyes begin to sting as she followed Reece to where a group of firemen were working.

They were prising open the doors to the lift shaft. One last heave and they gave, opening into darkness. She heard Reece curse under his breath. The floor of the lift was barely eight inches from the top of the doors.

'All right. Looks as if we'll have to go in from the top.'

One of the firemen stood back, surveying the gap. 'No one's getting out through there.'

'If we can get the inner doors open, at least we can talk to the people inside. Maybe give them some help if they need it.' Reece spoke up and the fireman swung round. 'We're medics.'

The fireman nodded, and Reece helped him to sweep the display from a raised dais and drag the dais over to the mouth of the lift. 'Okay. The engineer says that the lift's not going anywhere, so it's safe to reach through if you can get your arm in there.' Together, they prised the inner doors open.

Voices came from inside the lift and, almost in slow motion, a woman's hand reached out, as if somehow she could grasp the freedom of the open space outside.

'Okay. It's okay.' Reece took the woman's hand, in his, guiding it back inside the lift. 'There's been a fire but it's out now, and there's nothing more to worry about. The fire service is working to get you out. I'm a doctor. Is anyone hurt in there?'

'Yes. There's a man who fell when the lift stopped, he says he thinks he's sprained his wrist.'

'No one else?' Reece was craning to see inside the lift, and Sara handed him a torch.

'No, I don't think so. It's dark in here.'

'Here.' He handed his torch through to the woman inside the lift, and Sara passed him another. He turned to her.

'I can't get my arm through. Can you try?'

Sara stripped off the bulky jerkin and her coat, throwing them onto the floor. 'Give me a leg up.'

He bent down, half lifting her up onto the dais. Sara reached into the lift, finding that she could easily slip her shoulder inside.

'Good work.' Reece grinned at her. 'I'll pass anything

you need up to you, and if you can do your best to see inside…' He jumped down from their perch and opened the bag of medical supplies, checking to see what was there.

Sara stretched her neck to get some kind of view. Feet, and then a woman's face, her cheek pressed to the floor of the lift.

'Hey, there.' Sara grinned at her. 'My name's Sara, I'm a paramedic. How many are you?'

'Five. Two men, three women. I'm Claire.' The woman had obviously emerged as the leader of the small group, and she was doing her best to look after the others, even though she was plainly frightened.

'You're doing great, Claire. I want everyone to sit down on the floor, please…' There was room enough in the large lift, and the air would be clearer lower down. 'Now, I need to see everyone.'

'Right. The torch beam jumped, seeking out its target. 'This is David, he's hurt his hand.'

From what Sara could see, David probably hadn't just sprained his wrist. He was sitting on the floor, cradling a swollen hand, his face drawn. He gave a tight grin and a nod. 'Okay, David, hold on there for just a minute and I'll get back to you. What about the others?' She needed to see everyone first to assess her priorities.

Claire shone the light at each of the others in turn. Hannah, a young woman who was unhurt but worried about her baby, whom she had left with her sister on the ground floor. A young girl, Becky, who was pale and quiet but otherwise seemed okay, and pronounced herself to be fine. Mike, who was dressed in the uniform of a store assistant. Then Claire herself, middle-aged and capable.

'That's good. The firefighters are working above us to get you out of here. As far as I know, everyone got out of the store, but we'll see what we can find out about Hannah's family.' Sara twisted round.

'I saw a woman with a baby outside. She had a green coat. Redhead.' Reece was standing right behind her. 'The baby was crying, that's why I noticed them.'

'Hannah? Does your sister have red hair and a green coat?' Hannah's face brightened and she nodded. 'Okay, we think she's outside and she's got your baby with her.' She could hear Reece behind her, talking to one of the firemen. 'We're going to radio through and check.'

Sara turned back towards Reece. 'There's a guy in here called Mike, who works for the store. The firefighters might be looking for him, if he was noted as missing when they did the employee roll call.'

'Okay, we're on it.' Reece signalled to the fireman standing next to him, who was listening intently to the chatter on his radio.

Sara gave a tentative breath of relief. No major casualties. Nobody seemed to be panicking. So far so good. She flipped the beam of her torch back to David. 'Right. Let's take a look at that hand of yours.'

Claire helped David to slide to the front of the lift, and he gingerly held his hand out for her to examine. 'Did you hit your head when you fell? Feel dizzy at all, or sick?'

'No, no and yes.' David coughed, wincing as he did so. 'It's just the smoke in here.'

'Yeah.' Sara could identify with that. The smoke was beginning to get to the back of her throat and her eyes were stinging, but fresh air was filtering into the lift and the fine mist inside was clearing. 'Well, I don't think that's just a sprain, you may have broken a couple of the small bones in your hand. I want you to try and keep it still and we'll sort out a sling for you to make it easier for you to climb. Don't try hanging on with that hand, get the firemen to help you.'

'Right. Thanks.' David grinned at her. 'Don't suppose...' He broke off as a painful, laboured wheeze came from the other side of the lift car.

# CHAPTER SIXTEEN

SARA flipped the torch around in the direction of the sound, and its beam confirmed her fears. Becky was slumped forward, her head almost touching her knees, battling for air.

'We need to get out of here. Now!' Mike, the store assistant, chose this moment to try and assert himself, pushing past David and jamming his contorted face as close to Sara's as he could.

'Get back. I can't help her with you in the way.' Sara snapped out the order, hoping that the firmness of her tone would be enough to calm him. It was all she had. A girl could be dying just feet away and in front of her very eyes, and she could do nothing other than hope that the people who could reach her would stay calm and respond to her instructions.

Mike lunged back into the corner of the lift, his shoulders shaking with emotion, and Sara turned her attention back to Becky. 'Becky, do you have asthma? Nod if you can't speak.'

The teenager nodded, her chest heaving, and Claire scooted over to Sara. 'What do we do?'

'Support her in an upright sitting position. It's really important for you to be calm and reassure her. Get someone to look in her bag and you look in her pockets, you need to find her inhaler. Do it quickly.' Sara spoke quietly so that Becky wouldn't hear. She had no time to turn and ask for Reece's help, and he could do nothing more than she could. She could feel him there behind her, though, and that steadied her.

'Right.' Claire did as she was told, passing the teenager's handbag to Hannah, who started to fish around inside it.

'Quickly, Hannah.' She wasn't going to get anywhere with the large bag just dipping her hand in and feeling around. 'Empty it out…carefully…'

Hannah had tipped the bag upside down in a jerky movement and its contents went everywhere. The inhaler bounced and rolled across the floor and Sara made a grab for it, almost toppling off her perch as it spun towards her, out of the lift and downwards. Reece's hands on her waist stopped her from falling and she spun round to see where the inhaler had gone.

He was down in the lift pit in one beat of her heart. He found the inhaler amongst the debris at the bottom of the lift shaft and then Sara breathed again as he swung himself out from under the lift. 'I'm going upstairs. Perhaps I can get down there.' Before Sara could even nod, he was running towards the escalator.

Sara passed the inhaler back inside the lift and willing hands transferred it to Claire, who was sitting next to the Becky, supporting her. 'How do I use this?' She turned the inhaler over in her hand.

'Just give it to her. She knows how to use it, let her do it herself.' Sara nodded as the teenager took the inhaler and used it. Her breathing seemed to ease a little and Claire held her, comforting her. 'Good. That's good. Well done.'

It was medicine at arm's length. It was unbearably frustrating that she couldn't even touch her patient, but it seemed to be working. She flipped her eyes across to where Mike was sitting in the corner, and saw that David was talking quietly to him, his uninjured hand laid on his shoulder in a loose gesture of camaraderie. She grinned at David, and he winked back at her.

They weren't out of the woods yet, though. The sooner Reece could get to Becky and find a way of getting her out of the smoky atmosphere the better.

A couple of thuds, which seemed to come from the ceiling of the lift car, and everyone looked up expectantly. Everyone apart from Sara, who was still staring at Becky, trying to assess the rapid rise and fall of her chest and willing her to breathe. A small, hopeful murmur of excitement ran around the car as the ceiling hatch opened and a pair of legs appeared.

'It's okay, sweetheart. You're going to be fine, the doctor's with you now,' Sara called to Becky, and thought she saw some reaction.

Reece lowered himself into the lift, grinning, and Sara left her post. Now that he was there, he would do what was necessary, and there were things in the medical bag that he could use.

'Oxygen?' When she climbed back up to the opening, he was sitting next to the teenager, supporting her. He didn't look in her direction and Sara wondered whether the same radar that had told her that he had her back was operating for him.

'Here.' She slid the portable oxygen kit over to him and he reached for it.

A brief grin. Just enough to let her know that she was showing up bright and clear on his radar. 'Thanks.'

He unrolled the kit with one hand, giving the mask to the teenager to hold, while Claire shone the torch so he could see. 'Okay, sweetheart.' He guided the mask to the Becky's face. 'This will help you. You know what to do.'

His gaze met Sara's for a moment. The teenager was

responding, but not as much as either of them was happy with. Wordlessly, Sara slid the epi-pen and the intubation kit towards him, and he nodded. Just in case. There was no need to frighten their patient any further by voicing the need for them, but if it got to those last resorts, Reece might need them quickly.

'Well done, Becky. You're doing well.' He was holding her tenderly, reassuring her every step of the way. Almost coaxing the breaths from her, willing the blocked airway to clear, so that life-giving oxygen could reach her lungs. Sara tore her gaze away from them. This was no time to be thinking about Reece, or how she wanted some of that tenderness. Some of that reassurance that everything was going to be okay.

Turning to David, she smiled at him. 'How are you doing?'

'We're okay here.' His eyes slid to one side, towards Mike, who was sitting quietly now. 'See to the girl.'

'The doctor's got that under control. How's the hand now?'

'I've got a spare one, I can climb out if I need to.' Along with the others in the lift car, David had clearly divined what the next step was going to be.

'Sure you can. How's the pain?' It was a delicate balance. Sara would have had no hesitation in administering pain relief straight away in normal circumstances, but David still needed to focus. Too much pain would rob him of that focus, but so would too many drugs.

'It hurts.'

'I can give you pain relief, but you need to keep your wits about you.'

David grinned at her. 'I'll keep my wits for the moment. When I get out of here, you can give me as many drugs as you like.'

'Me too,' Mike piped up, and then quietened down again when Sara ignored him.

'David, I'm going to pass you through a sling and the doctor will put it on for you. It'll make it easier when they come to getting you out.' It was obvious from the sounds of activity going on above them that the fire crew was working on creating a safe passage upwards and out of the lift.

'Don't bother him. I can manage.'

'I'll help you.' Hannah slid over towards Sara, taking the sling when she passed it through, and gently slipping it over David's head, fixing it as Sara told her to. He winced with pain and then relaxed.

'Is that better?'

'Much. Thanks.' His head snapped round as the sound of wheezing came from the other side of the lift car. Reece was reaching for the teenager's inhaler again.

'Hannah, get that piece of paper, will you?' Sara indicated a scrap of paper in the pile from the teenager's handbag. 'Roll it up…a bit tighter than that… Yes, that's right.'

'Thanks.' Reece took the rolled-up paper, using it as a makeshift spacer between the inhaler and the teenager's mouth. It would keep the medicine in place between breaths, and what Becky needed right now, more than anything else, was her medication. 'Breathe now, sweetheart.'

Becky's hand found Reece's arm, tightening around it. She was hanging on, as if the mere fact of holding onto him would help her to breathe. 'That's right. Squeeze my arm when you're ready to take another breath.'

The tips of her fingers whitened as she squeezed hard, and Reece worked the inhaler again. 'That's right. You're doing beautifully. Two more puffs.'

The wheezing had stopped again and Reece was gently replacing the oxygen mask. 'Better now?' Becky nodded, and something that looked like a smile ghosted across her lips.

A ladder dropped down through the hatch in the ceiling, and a fireman climbed down, bringing with him the harness that would be needed to get Becky out. Another fireman appeared and started to marshal the other occupants of the lift up the ladder, one by one, while Reece helped to strap the teenager into the harness.

'We're on our way up.' He gripped Becky's hand, in a signal that she wasn't going anywhere without him, and she managed a grin. 'That's the ticket.' He smiled back, and the fireman connected the harness to a cable, ready to winch their patient upwards.

'Sara…' The one word betrayed him. He may have been working without even looking her way most of the time, but it didn't mean that he hadn't known that she'd been there. At times like these, ignoring someone, letting them get on with their job, was the deepest form of trust.

'I'll meet you upstairs.' Sara scrambled down from her perch, shouldering the straps of the heavy kitbag, and made for the escalator as quickly as the darkness and the weight of the bag would allow.

The muscles in her legs were screaming for mercy by the time she got to the top, but she didn't stop. The smoke in the basement and in the lift shaft had been clearing as it had drifted upwards, but here it was still heavy in the air. Reece had already freed Becky from the harness and hoisted her up in his arms, hurrying towards the exit.

Dropping the bag, Sara ran ahead of him towards the open shop doors. 'Coming through,' she yelled at the group of people between them and the waiting ambulance. There was no less urgency now, in the cold air, than there had been in the smoky atmosphere. Reece made the back of the ambulance, and waiting hands guided them both inside.

The doors closed in her face and Sara stared at them. She should go back, collect the bag and check on how the others were doing, but something stopped her. She needed to see Reece. Just for one moment.

The doors opened again and he stepped down from the ambulance. The smile on his face told her all she needed to know. 'She's okay?'

He nodded. 'Now that she's out of there, she's breathing a lot more easily. I told her I'd go with her to the hospital. Will you see if you can find my jacket? It's by the lift opening on the ground floor.'

'Of course. There's some more for me to do here, but I'll meet you there.'

He nodded, his blue eyes flashing with something that looked like relief. If there had been no unfinished business between them before, now there was plenty. Being parted from him now, after they'd done so much together today, was like having one of her arms wrenched off.

'Thanks. Only I don't know where we're going.'

'I do. Wait in the coffee bar on the east wing for me.'

'Sure. See you later.' He climbed back into the ambulance, closing the doors, and she lost sight of him.

She found Reece where she'd told him to wait, sitting in the cafeteria, half a cup of coffee in front of him.

'Hey, there. How are you doing?'

'Fine. How's Becky?'

Reece grinned. 'They're keeping her in overnight, but she's okay. I saw David come into A and E too. Four broken bones in his hand. They're splinting it and sending him home.'

'That's good. I checked everyone else over and they're fine.' Sara grinned. 'Hannah's little boy is a real sweetheart.'

His gaze caught hers and they locked. Held. The way they had back at his house in Australia. The way she had relived in her dreams ever since, and had tried so hard to avoid in the last twenty-four hours.

'Are you going to finish your coffee?'

He shook his head. 'No. I do have to pay for it, though. When I got here I realised I'd left my wallet in my jacket, and I had to beg for credit. One pound twenty. I had a bun as well.'

Sara got her purse out, leaning towards him. 'So how did you get Irene to give you credit?' The lady who ran the Friends' Coffee Bar was a treasure. A very stern treasure who made it an unbreakable rule never, ever to give credit.

'She was very nice about it. I explained what had happened and said that you'd be along to rescue me any time now, and she gave me one free cup of coffee and then came over and took an IOU from me for a second cup and a bun.' He was smiling now. His shock of blond hair and mischievous eyes told Sara exactly how he'd managed to get Irene to break her unbreakable rule. He'd just charmed her into it.

'You got a free cup of coffee?' Sara whispered the words at him in case anyone overheard and started a rumour.

'I'm not supposed to tell anyone.' He looked over his shoulder furtively. 'Perhaps you should give me the money and wait for me outside while I go and pay.'

'Okay.' Sara pressed a coin into his hand and he squinted at it. 'There's two pounds. Meet me outside and we'll go back to my place and I'll make you a decent cup of coffee.'

'I'll just get my jacket from your car and then I've got to get going.' The refusal of her invitation felt like a slap in the face and Sara reminded herself that just last night it had been her telling Reece to go. 'But I was wondering if you were free tomorrow.'

'Yes…' She'd answered before she had bothered to think. 'Why?'

'Thought you might like to do something. I've got a tourist guide and an Oyster card.' He made it all sound so innocent.

She should say no. On the other hand, he hadn't abandoned her when she'd been alone in Australia. And they did need to talk. Perhaps he was right, and it would be better to do that after a night's sleep. 'Okay. Where do you want to go?'

'I don't know yet. Any ideas?'

Sara thought for a moment. 'I'll meet you at Green Park Station. Come up onto street level and I'll meet you by the exit on the same side of the road as the park. Can you get there all right?'

He nodded. 'I'll find it. What time?'

'One o'clock. I'll go and see Gran in the morning and I'll take you to lunch.'

'No.'

'No?' The ends of her fingertips began to tingle. They'd had this conversation before, hadn't they?

'My shout.' He grinned, getting up and making for the serving hatch to pay Irene before she had a chance to argue.

# CHAPTER SEVENTEEN

'So, WHAT do you think? Do you like it here?'

That was his line surely. Then Reece remembered where he was and realised that he was the tourist, not Sara. You'd never have known it from the way she'd been acting but, then, Reece had learned something today. Back in Australia, he'd thought that her keen interest in everything around her had been because her surroundings had been new to her, but he'd been wrong. She was like that all the time.

'Yeah.' He weighed up the pros and cons, finding it impossible to compare this with his homeland. 'Yes, it's... different.'

She laughed. 'Cold?'

'Yes, cold. I assume you do get a summer?'

'Course we do.' They'd stopped walking, and the stiff breeze from the river was making her cheeks flush pink. 'Most years.'

He laughed. Free and clear, allowing his chest to expand and take in air. It seemed so much easier to do that when Sara was around. 'It's amazing.' The London Eye towered to one side of them, turning so slowly that it was impossible to track. All the same, it turned, and in the space of half an hour passengers got a full three-hundred-and-sixty-degree view. 'Such a lot to see.'

'That's why I made you walk. It's much better than just going from place to place on the Tube.'

She'd made him walk all right. And after the exertions of yesterday and a broken night's sleep, he was beginning to ache. But it had been worth it, and Reece had felt he'd seen the best of the city, glittering proudly under a cold, clear sky. Or maybe it just seemed that way because Sara was there.

A thought struck him, and suddenly he couldn't get it out of his head. As they'd walked across Westminster Bridge together, she'd told him about how gold rings and coins, centuries old, were washed up on the shores of the river. 'Will you stay there for a moment? I just want to go back onto the bridge to get a photograph of the river.'

'Hmm? Yes, of course.' Her attention had been diverted by a pavement artist, who was putting the finishing touches to a chalked image. 'I'm just going to go and see what this guy's doing.'

Reece strode back onto the bridge, walking almost to the centre of it. This was the place. Turning, he saw Sara raise her head and wave, as if she knew that he was looking at her. He waved back and he thought he saw her smile.

Training his camera lens up the river, he took a couple of shots, managing to get one of the Houses of Parliament with a red bus going past. Then, reaching into his pocket almost furtively, his fingers found the gold chain with the small heart threaded onto it that had travelled with him ever since he had failed to give it to Sara.

It was time to let go of this. He'd brought it with him, thinking that a goodbye was the only thing that they had left to do. Maybe that was true and maybe it wasn't. He could no longer hold himself to it, though. His relationship with Sara was too multi-textured, too full of possibilities to bind himself to just one outcome. He had to let go.

Leaning on the wide parapet, looking out over the water, he let the bauble drop and it spun downwards, glittering in the low sun. He thought he saw it hang in the water for a moment before it sank, but perhaps that was just his imagination. Reece turned and walked back towards the bank, without looking back. One day the shifting waters would probably throw it back up onto the river shore again, but he would never know about it.

When he rejoined her, she was still studying the chalked image on the pavement. 'I guess it'll be getting dark soon.'

She looked at her watch. 'Yes.' She seemed to be turning something over in her mind. Probably the same thing he was. They could only pretend for so long that there was nothing more that needed to be said. 'We should talk, Reece.'

'Yes. We should.'

'My place?' The two words seemed like water to a dying man. He'd come here to find some way of breaking free, and yet the only time he felt free was when he was with Sara.

There really wasn't a choice in the matter. 'Yes. Your place.

The house was dark and quiet. Last night it had seemed unbearable, walking up the front path, with no glow from Gran's window to welcome her home. Sara had no plan. No idea what she was going to do next, whether she was going to let him stay the night in the spare room or call him a taxi after they'd eaten. She'd work that one out when she came to it.

Dropping her keys on the kitchen counter top, she made for the coffee-machine. 'Fancy a decent cup of coffee?'

'Love one.' He grinned. 'That's quite a magnificent beast you have there.'

'This?' She indicated her espresso machine. She'd never quite got the hang of which lever to pull when. 'My mother had this installed for when she entertained. She never used it, just got the catering staff to do the honours.'

'Did she entertain a lot?'

'A fair bit. Only ever for business. She reckoned it was easier to talk people into things over a meal, a decent vintage and properly brewed espresso.' Sara watched as coffee dripped into the cups.

'Probably right. Only if you brew your espresso for that long, it'll be bitter.'

Sara kept her back turned to him, so he couldn't see her grin. 'Oh, and so you're an expert, are you? The man with no coffee beans in his cupboard and a grinder that needed to be excavated before it would work.'

'Just because I don't drink decent coffee, it doesn't mean to say I don't know how to make it.' His voice was closer now, and a bead of cool sweat ran down her spine. 'I had a part-time job as a barista when I was at uni. Little place in Melbourne where they used to do speciality coffees.'

'So you can probably show me where I'm going wrong, then.' She kept her eyes doggedly on the machine.

'Yeah. We'll have to start again, though, right from the beginning.' He fetched the milk from the refrigerator while Sara knocked the grounds from the filters into the bin.

His arms reached around her, picking up the tin of coffee beans that she'd taken out of the cupboard. All she had to do was to lean back a little and she'd be touching him. It would be the sweetest, most delicious thing that she could imagine.

He kept her in front of him, inside the circle of his arms, while he ground the coffee and filled the filters, tamping them down just so hard and no more. 'Your espresso needs to be filtered for less than a minute, any longer and it gets bitter. So start with the milk.' He moved away from her for a moment to froth the milk, signalling to her when the time was right to press the brew button. Then he whipped the cups out from under the filters and put the milk jug in front of her.

'Now I have to hit it, yes?' She could feel him again. His body against hers, his fingertips resting on the counter top on either side of her.

'No, you tap firmly. Don't bash the jug down as if you're trying to beat it to death.' Sara tapped the jug on the counter top to settle the milk and he laughed softly. 'Bit harder than that. Three times.'

'Three?'

'Yeah. I always do it three times.'

Somehow he made that sound like a proposition. Sara swallowed hard, and tapped. 'Very good. Now tip the cup to coat the inside with coffee.' He reached for one of the cups, showing her what he meant, and Sara did the same with the other. 'And tip the milk in slowly. That's right.' He waited for her to tip the milk into both cups. 'All you need now is chocolate sprinkles.'

'Hmm. Think I'm out of sprinkles.' She summoned up the courage to turn and face him. It was just as she'd thought. His eyes, dark and delicious. His body taut. And that smile was just downright dangerous.

He shook his head. 'What about amaretti biscuits? Something sweet to go with the coffee.'

'Sorry. None of those either.'

'Too bad.' He was so very close. 'Guess I'll just have to go to the source.'

He kissed her. Lightly on the lips. Warm. She could feel his warmth, tingling through her body. They'd gone too far already, but all Sara could think was that it wasn't far enough.

'Hmm. Perfect.' He kissed her again, and this time she felt his hands, laid lightly on her hips. It was too late to do anything now other than just enjoy this moment. And the next.

'It's chilly in here…' Sara hadn't changed the thermostats on the radiators yet, and Gran's flat was probably as warm as toast, while up here the heating was turned down low.

'Yeah. And I don't know about you but I'm starting to ache like hell.'

There were two ways of taking that. Probably both pretty accurate right now. Sara's legs ached from the stairs yesterday and the long walk today, and the rest of her… The rest of her just ached for him. 'I've got the very thing for that. Bring your coffee.'

She took him upstairs to the big master bathroom. She normally used the en suite shower in her bedroom, reckoning that the big spa tub was no good for just one person, but now it was just perfect.

'Not quite sure how this works.' She fiddled with the levers. 'I've never used it before.'

'Let me.' He set the temperature and twisted one of the taps, setting hot water gushing into the tub. 'Now, anything else I can help you with?'

They floated together in the warm bubbles, his arms wrapped around her shoulders. Slowly they were pushing the boundaries, taking one at a time. At first they'd just looked and not touched. Now they were touching, without caressing.

'Are you sure that you live here?' Reece was staring ruminatively at the ceiling.

'Yeah. Course I do.'

'It's just that you don't seem to know how anything works in this house.' He stroked the side of her face with his finger. 'I was just wondering whether the real owners were going to come home any minute and ask what we're doing here.'

Underneath the lightness of his tone was a serious point. One that Sara had wrestled with for a while now. 'It's never really been my home. Bit too much like a show home for my taste.'

'Hmm. It's not the kind of place I'd imagine you living.'

'No. I don't imagine me living here either. But for the foreseeable future…'

'You'll stay here because your gran's flat is here. And if you sell this place, you won't be able to bring her home.'

He understood that, at least. 'Yes. It's not the home that I chose, but it's where I've ended up.'

'Where would you rather be?' He said it as if there was a choice.

'I've got a cottage of my own. Not as posh as this, all the furniture's secondhand and it's small and some way out of London, but it was mine.'

'Not any more?'

'I'm going to sell it. It's stupid to keep two places on, and I was going to send the money to Simon. My mother left everything to me, but I don't want it. He should have something.' She'd hung onto her own place way too long now in the hope that somehow she would be able to return. It just wasn't practical, though. It was too small to give Gran a decent-sized bedroom and sitting room on the ground floor, and the money would come in handy for Simon.

'You could make this place yours.' He seemed to be considering something. 'You made my place into a home and you were only there for two weeks.'

Did he really think that? When she'd left Reece's house, it had felt like leaving her own home, but she hadn't realised that he'd felt it too. As if somehow what they'd shared there had seeped into the bricks and mortar of the place, making it special.

She didn't really want to think too much about that. 'Yeah. You'll be moving on soon, though.'

'I have already.'

'Moving on for good, I mean. You're like one of those fish that suffocates if they stop swimming.'

'I think you mean a shark.' He splashed some water in her direction.

'Or a tuna. You could be a tuna if you preferred.'

He snorted, obviously unimpressed with the choice. 'I'll let you know.' He pulled her into his arms, and the water rocked in the tub. It seemed that the ban on caressing was now over. 'In the meantime, what about those aches and pains?'

'Still a little achy.'

'Hmm. Want me to rub them better?'

Reece had hardly noticed the decor when he had carried her into her bedroom, making a wrong turn out of the bathroom and having to get her to point the way. He hadn't noticed anything much, other than the deep hunger that penetrated his bones and left him unable to do anything other than just what he was doing now. Making love to her. Holding her in his arms while they merged into what seemed like one being. Moving as one. Feeling as one.

When he woke up, though, some time in the middle of the night, light streaming through the open door from the hallway, he did notice. The walls were painted a shade of rich caramel instead of the bright white of the rest of the house. Wooden furniture and soft earth shades on the curtains and bedspread. Sara's unique way of blending colour and texture, the way she'd arranged the iridescent, polished agates on her dresser, which made the room soft and welcoming. The rest of the house was about as welcoming as an ice hotel.

She appeared, holding a glass of water. Still naked, even though she was shivering slightly from the cold air outside the room.

'Come back to bed.' The words felt possessive. Greedy for the endless possibilities that they held. Reece had wondered whether his memory had been taunting him by enhancing the delights of making love with Sara. It hadn't. If anything, it had left a few things out.

'Sorry. Did I wake you?' She scooted across the room and dumped the water on the bedside table, before sliding in beside him.

'No. Ow—your hands are cold! And your feet. What on earth have you been doing?'

'I went downstairs to get some water and put your clothes in the washing machine. They were in a soggy pile on the bathroom floor.'

'So I can't leave, then?'

'They'll be dry by the morning. It's a washer-drier, runs on an automatic cycle.'

Clean, dry clothes, so he could leave in the morning. There were times when her practicality was downright distressing. 'Okay. Guess that means that I'll have to make the best of my time, then.' There wasn't really a great deal of choice in the matter. Her hands were sliding up his thighs, deliciously cold, leaving trails of pure desire in their wake.

'You like that?'

'Love it. That's one thing this climate has in its favour.' The cosy warmth of her bed. The tantalising coldness of her fingers against his skin, tracing their way lightly towards his groin. 'No...wait, Sara...'

She didn't listen to him, and sudden pleasure gripped him, pulling tight on his senses. 'No?' She was teasing him now, and pure delight shot through his body, turning his blood to fire and making his eyes snap upwards in their sockets

A low growl escaped his throat, and he tipped her over onto her back, covering her with his bulk. The primitive male in him surfaced, revelling in her softness, the slim lines of her frame, clamouring to take her for his own. 'Come here…'

She giggled, letting out a squeal as he pulled her legs around his waist, goading him further by planting her cold feet right in the small of his back. 'No, you come here…'

Sara woke to find herself locked tight in his arms, his body curved around hers. That was fine. Right now, the last thing she wanted to do was move.

When he woke up, he made coffee for them both, and they lay together, talking. She planned out his stay in London, suggesting things to see, places that he could go that were off the usual tourist circuit. He redesigned her house, suggesting she throw out the white leather sofas in the lounge and replace them with the warm, earth tones that she loved.

'I can't. They're designer sofas, my mother paid a fortune for them.'

'Do you ever sit on them?'

'No. If I want to sit down, I either sit with Gran or I come up here.' She indicated the easy chair in the corner of the room, next to her books.

'So they've already gone to waste.' He shrugged. 'I imagine you could sell them then someone else will appreciate and use them.'

He had a point. If she sold them, she'd probably be able to redecorate the whole room with the proceeds. But something in the back of her mind wanted to revolt against that logic, turn it on its head. Why make this place look like a home, when really it wasn't? She'd never wanted to come back here, and now that Gran was gone, the only thing that made it feel like home was Reece. And he would be gone soon, and whatever colour the walls were, or however many soft furnishings she changed, the place would still be sterile and unwelcoming.

'I guess.' It was time to get out of bed now. Time to face the things that she'd been so unwilling to face last night. 'Your clothes will be dry now, and I really should move if I'm going to see Gran this afternoon.' She looked at the clock. It *was* already this afternoon. 'Would you like me to print out some information from the Internet for you? About the places I told you…?'

She couldn't go on. It hurt too much. The look of reproach in his eyes seared through her like a red-hot knife.

'So you're not going to do any more sightseeing with me, then?'

Sara reached for her thick dressing gown and pulled it on then perched herself on the edge of the linen chest at the foot of the bed. 'No. I don't think I am.'

He nodded slowly. 'Is there anything I can do to change your mind?'

Everything he did changed her mind, that was the problem. 'I think we've just proved that being friends doesn't really work with us. We just end up…' She couldn't say it.

'We end up here. Is that so terrible?'

She couldn't look him in the eye. Whatever she found there, it would be enough to stop her from doing this. 'We've done everything that we can do, Reece. There's no future in this, and I want to say goodbye now, before things start to go bad between us.'

'And that's what you really want?' If he felt anything, he was giving none of it away. His face was like a mask, suddenly devoid of emotion. None of the disbelief and exasperation that he'd shown when he'd asked her to stay in Australia and she'd said she couldn't. None of the sheer, bloody-minded determination to sweep all her objections aside when he'd arrived the night before last.

'You and I are different creatures, Reece. We live differently, and neither of us can change who we are.' She was going to cry in a minute. She had to get out of here before she fell into his arms, sobbing and pleading for one more day. Another night. One more moment, even.

He didn't move. Didn't even try to argue with her. Sara stood up, feeling the muscles in her legs pull as she did so.

'I'll always care for you, Sara.' She had almost reached the door before he spoke.

'Thank you.' She didn't turn and face him, afraid of what she might reveal. Afraid of what he might see in her eyes. 'I know.'

It was like a landslide. It had started so suddenly, and now that it had gathered momentum it was unstoppable. Merciless in its swift path, flattening everything as it went. He showered and dressed in less than ten minutes, and two minutes later he'd put his jacket on, picking his wallet up from the kitchen counter where he'd left it last night. Checking his pockets to make sure he'd left nothing behind, so he wouldn't have to come back.

'I'll hold you in my heart, Sara.'

It was what Kath had said at the airport, but he'd left a bit out. *Until I see you again.* Sara bit her lip. Sensible. That wasn't going to happen. She put her hand over her heart, the way she'd done with Kath. 'I'll hold you in my heart too, Reece.' Maybe one day she'd see him again. In about a thousand years' time, when there was no question of her wanting him any more.

He kissed her on the cheek, turning quickly. Maybe he

didn't want to see her tears any more than she wanted to show them to him. Sara squeezed her eyes shut, wrapping her arms tightly around herself, until she heard the front door close.

'No.' Suddenly she couldn't believe what she'd done. Running to the door, she pulled it open, only just remembering to grab her keys. Barefoot and still clad only in her dressing gown, she ran up the front path, her feet stinging from the frost on the pavers.

She caught sight of him, striding away. As he turned the corner she thought he would look back, but he didn't. It was only then that she realised that she didn't know the name of the hotel he was staying at and for one giddy moment she knew that if she ran after him, he wouldn't ignore her and just keep walking.

It wasn't the freezing weather or her bare feet that deterred her. It was the ice around her heart. If she stopped him now, she would just face this moment again and again, until finally the pain of parting obliterated everything else. Sara turned and walked back into the house, closing the door behind her. She was ready to cry now. At least she could do that.

# CHAPTER EIGHTEEN

IT HAD been a tough week. For the first few days Sara had slept in the tiny spare room in Gran's apartment, along with Gran's collection of porcelain dogs and a stack of boxes of things that were no longer used but couldn't possibly be thrown away. She'd ventured up to her own room for long enough to strip the bed and open the windows to the freezing air, in the hope that this might erase the memories that Reece had made. It was no use. However hard she tried not to think about him, he was still there, in the very air that she breathed.

Three days' work had at least diverted her attention slightly, although the evenings were still as empty and sorrowful. And a thick fall of snow on Friday had occupied her in clearing the sloping drive that led to the house, so that she could get her car up to the front door when she bought Gran home on Saturday morning.

'Who built the snowman?' Sara put on a smile for the carer who answered the door and gestured towards the large snowman built outside the window so the residents could see it when they passed on the way to the dining room.

'Oh, one of the relatives. The gardener helped as well, I think.'

'It's nice.' One of the things that Sara liked about this

place was that practically anything was cause for celebration. A birthday, a public holiday, a fall of snow. Everything was marked by as much joy as the care staff could manage to inject into it. 'Is Gran in her room?'

'No, she's in the small sitting room, playing bridge.'

'At eleven o'clock in the morning?' A thought struck Sara. 'She hasn't been up all night playing, has she?' Gran had a habit of sleeping during the day and then sitting up till late at night.

'We had to make her go to bed. And the card sharps got together again this morning for a last game.'

'Right. Thanks.' Sara supposed that she would have to wait, at least until this rubber was finished. That was okay, she had nothing else to do.

She called in on Gran, and then went upstairs to her room to pack her things for the weekend. Opening the door, she thought she caught a hint of Reece's scent. Her senses had been playing those cruel tricks on her all week.

'Hey, Sara.'

She dropped her car keys, and they jangled onto the carpet. Tried to gulp in a breath of air, and failed. 'What are you doing here, Reece?'

'Lily said I could wait here for you.'

In some ways, it was a worse intrusion than if he'd shinned up the drainpipe, climbed in through the window and settled himself down in Gran's easy chair. 'What, so you took advantage of a ninety-year-old woman to…?' To see her. He could only have done it to see her. Sara tried to not to think about it. She didn't need to feel that kind of joy, not right now.

'No.' He stood up. Stiff, uncertain. Formal somehow. 'I told Lily that I wanted to see you.'

'What did you have to go upsetting Gran for?' The blood

had started to pump around her body again now, and Sara felt her cheeks flush. Maybe it was just the heat in here.

'It wasn't like that, Sara. I dropped in during the week with the photos of Simon that I promised her the other day.'

Sara bit her lip. He had promised the photos, and she knew how much Gran wanted them. All the same, he shouldn't have told Gran about their personal business. 'And, what, you just happened to convince her that this was a good idea?'

'She asked me if she would see me at the weekend and I said no. This was her idea.'

It just got worse and worse. Her own grandmother was conspiring with her ex-lover. 'Right. Well, you've seen me. You and Gran have both got what you wanted, so you can go now.'

'There's something I want to tell you. I can tell you now, or I can meet you later and tell you. Any time and any place you like.' It sounded like someone arranging to meet for coffee, but this was unmistakeably an ultimatum. The tension in Reece's tone, the tightness in his face left Sara in no doubt that he would catch up with her sooner or later.

She sighed. This was turning into a nightmare of goodbyes. The first had been bad enough and the second had almost torn her apart. She doubted that this one would be any better. 'Look, we can't talk here.' She couldn't take Gran home when she was in this state either. She'd better get it over and done with. 'We'll take a walk. Outside in the garden.' Maybe the cold would encourage him to keep this short.

'Okay.' He caught his jacket up from the back of the chair and put it on. Wound a thick scarf around his neck and put on a pair of gloves. He'd learned one thing, at least, during the course of the week.

The cold outside hit her full in the face, and she snuggled

into her warm, padded coat. The thought struck her that she'd worn this coat not just because of its warmth but because it was red. Something to make her look a little more cheery for when she saw Gran.

'Do you like the snowman?'

'Yes, it's great, isn't it?' Sara answered before the significance of the question struck her. 'Is this your handiwork?'

He grinned suddenly. Just for a moment before that tense, solemn look returned to his face. 'I'm a tourist. Can't resist a little snow.' He trudged along the path that led around the building, taking care to walk where other people had already left their footsteps. Like a child who didn't want to spoil the pristine white of the undisturbed snow.

Sara waited. He'd wanted this, not her. She wasn't going to ask what it was all about, that would sound as if she wanted to know.

'I want to buy your cottage.'

'You can't.' If that was all it was, the answer was simple. 'I've already got an offer on it. Came in last week. Full asking price.'

'And you've accepted the offer?'

'Yes, I have.'

'Good.' He was kicking at the snow with the toe of his boot, not looking at her.

'Is that all?'

'You're going to throw in the carpets and curtains as well?' He looked up at her suddenly, and the full force of his blue eyes hit her. Like an iceberg, smashing against her, dragging her under.

'You… Reece, you didn't.'

'I'm afraid I did.' He wasn't afraid at all. He'd decided to do it and had just gone ahead and done it. She knew him well enough to know that.

'So you've been poking around in my cottage, have

you?' Suddenly the thought of him there was more than she could bear.

'The estate agent phoned and asked you first.'

'Yes, but she didn't say that it was you who wanted to look around.'

He nodded, turning the edges of his mouth downwards. 'No, she didn't. I told her that I didn't want her to give anyone my name until I was ready to make an offer on a property.'

'Right. So you trick your way into my house, and then make a cash offer. I suppose that's as bogus as you are.'

'Just because I don't own property, it doesn't mean to say I don't have savings.' He couldn't keep up the hurt look that he flashed her for very long and a grin started to spread over his face. 'In fact, it looks as if the two are mutually exclusive—even small cottages don't come cheap.'

'I know how much my cottage costs. What are you planning on doing with it?' It was a theoretical question. She wasn't going to sell to Reece and that was that. Asking price or not.

'I'll need somewhere to live. I need a work permit and a job as well. I've got those in hand too.'

This was ridiculous. Some kind of mad gesture that was all going to come to grief in the end. 'No, you don't need a work permit because I'm not going to sell you my house and you're not getting a job. It'll just make everything much more complicated when you move on.'

'It will, won't it?' His forehead was creased with stress. She knew that look, and there was something he wasn't saying. 'Sara, you said that I'd suffocate if I stopped moving.'

'Yes. You would.' It was the truth, and he needed to see that before he made a mistake that would not just break her heart but break both their souls.

'Have you ever been to Mexico?'

'No.' She stamped her foot in frustration.

'I want to show you the Caves of the Sleeping Sharks in Isla Mujeres. The water there is so rich in oxygen that reef sharks rest motionless at the bottom of the caves. They don't need to stay swimming in order to breathe.'

She could feel her tears. Sara wondered whether they might freeze and stick to her face. 'That's just a story, Reece. It doesn't mean to say—'

'It does.' He turned on her with such certainty that she almost backed away from him. 'When you left Australia, I was just about to leave Victoria. I couldn't. I couldn't leave the house where you'd been, or the places we'd seen together. I was trapped, like a man in an underwater pocket of air, trying not to breathe too much. The only place I could come, the only place where I could breathe again, was here, with you.'

She stared at him. He really was serious about this.

'The only way that I can think of to show you that I'm serious about this is to just do it. I know you don't believe me now, but let me show you.'

'What, by nailing your feet to the floor, Reece? That's what buying property does. It's a commitment.'

His shoulders seemed to relax a little. 'Exactly. That's exactly what I'm doing, because I don't need to be anywhere else. You are all I want and everything that I need. If I have to nail my feet to the floor to show you that, then…' He grinned. 'Pass the hammer.'

'You don't know what you're doing, Reece. There's Gran to think about. I don't have time…' She trailed off. 'It's not fair to ask you to stay when I don't have the energy or the time to devote to a relationship. I tried that balancing act a long time ago, and I failed.'

He stopped short, looking at her with reproach in his eyes. Maybe she shouldn't have brought up the thing with

Tim. It wasn't the same at all. Reece wasn't the kind of guy who would sit on the sidelines, let her do all the work and then complain that she was never around.

'He was a fool, then. He didn't love you enough.' He threw the words at her, disgust in his voice.

'No…I suppose he didn't.' Some of Reece's no-holds-barred straightforwardness seemed to have rubbed off on her. 'And to tell you the truth, I probably didn't love him enough either. I love you, though, and that's why I'm not going to let you stay.'

'We'll look after Lily together.' He shrugged. 'If she'll have me.'

'Oh, she'll have you all right.' It was all or nothing now. She had to call his bluff. Sara didn't want to even think about his answer, but she had to know. 'Marry me, then.' She threw the challenge down, and it lay freezing at their feet.

She couldn't bear the shock in his eyes. 'Sara, I'm not ready…'

He'd done just what she'd thought he would, and yet had hoped against impossible hope that he wouldn't. Baulked at the last fence. There was nothing more to say. If this was what it took to make him realise that staying was just a crazy plan that he'd never be able to stick to then so be it. Sara turned and walked away from him.

'Wait.' He caught her arm and she pulled it away. There really was nothing left to say. 'Wait!' His tone was almost harsh, and his hand closed around her arm again, this time unyielding.

'Let me go.'

'Never.' He pulled her back towards him, banding his arms around her body, and she struggled vainly to get free. 'I'm not ready to ask you properly. I don't have a ring and I haven't wined and dined you yet in the best restaurant in town. I left all that until later, because I reckoned it might take me a while to prove myself to you.'

'You don't need to prove yourself. All I need is your word.'

'Then you have it.' He pulled her close and she felt his body relax along with her own. 'We'll get married by special licence.' He paused. 'Can you do that here?'

'We will not. I want a proper wedding, with Simon and Gran there. Do you think that we could get Kath and Joe to come over?'

He let out a short, barking laugh of disbelief. 'Try keeping her away. In fact, it'll be interesting to see how long she manages to hold out before she starts sending you cake ideas.'

'Sounds good. Be nice to have something a bit different. I want a beautiful dress and a cake…' She tipped her head upwards and kissed him. 'I want you.'

'You've got it. All of it, I promise.' He bent closer, his lips grazing her ear. 'I think we've got an audience.'

'Gran?' Sara didn't even look. Gran was safe and sound inside and this moment was hers.

'Yeah. Along with a growing crowd.' He chuckled. 'I may not have a ring but I've got witnesses.'

'Reece, what are you doing? Get up.' He'd fallen to his knees in the snow. 'You'll get wet and then you'll freeze to death.'

'Better answer me quickly, then.' He resisted all her attempts to pull him to his feet, and closed his hands around hers. 'I want to make a home with you, Sara. I want to fill it with all the love I can give you, and share that with Lily. I want to make babies, and have our children grow up knowing that there's a wonderful world out there but that there's a place where they can always come and find us…'

He stopped, searching her face. This was Reece all over.

When he made a promise he made it comprehensively, missing out nothing.

'Sounds wonderful.' Sara smiled at him, willing him on.

He nodded. 'I want to love you and make you happy. Will you marry me, Sara?'

He'd missed nothing out. 'Yes, Reece. I'll marry you.' She pulled him up, out of the freezing snow, and this time he made no effort to resist her, holding her tight against his chest and kissing her, to the faint, muffled sound of applause from the sitting-room window.

There was one thing she wanted, but Sara knew she couldn't have that. 'I want this to last for ever.'

'It will. It'll be in my heart, whenever you want it.'

He'd done the impossible. She could move now, instead of standing here shivering in the magic of the moment. She could walk away from it, knowing that Reece would be with her.

The sound of a sharp rapping on the window caught her attention. The senior carer was beckoning them. 'Ah. It's nearly time for morning coffee, and that looks like an invitation we can't refuse.'

He chuckled. 'Sounds like a plan. I'm losing the feeling in my fingers.'

She stripped off his glove, tucking his hand inside her coat. 'Better?'

'Much.' They started to walk together around the building, back to the main entrance.

'I guess this means the sale on my cottage just fell through.' She grinned up at him.

'Not necessarily. If you want to live there and Lily's happy with it, there's plenty of room at the back. We could build an extension for her, have it designed especially for her needs.'

She shrugged. 'It doesn't matter any more. We can clear the house out, make it ours. Plenty of space for visitors.'

He chuckled. 'I've a feeling we'll need it.' He turned to her, pulling her against the side wall of the building, out of sight of watchful eyes. 'Now, before we go and share, I want one more kiss.'

* * * * *

# Mills & Boon® Hardback

## February 2013

## ROMANCE

| | |
|---|---|
| **Sold to the Enemy** | Sarah Morgan |
| **Uncovering the Silveri Secret** | Melanie Milburne |
| **Bartering Her Innocence** | Trish Morey |
| **Dealing Her Final Card** | Jennie Lucas |
| **In the Heat of the Spotlight** | Kate Hewitt |
| **No More Sweet Surrender** | Caitlin Crews |
| **Pride After Her Fall** | Lucy Ellis |
| **Living the Charade** | Michelle Conder |
| **The Downfall of a Good Girl** | Kimberly Lang |
| **The One That Got Away** | Kelly Hunter |
| **Her Rocky Mountain Protector** | Patricia Thayer |
| **The Billionaire's Baby SOS** | Susan Meier |
| **Baby out of the Blue** | Rebecca Winters |
| **Ballroom to Bride and Groom** | Kate Hardy |
| **How To Get Over Your Ex** | Nikki Logan |
| **Must Like Kids** | Jackie Braun |
| **The Brooding Doc's Redemption** | Kate Hardy |
| **The Son that Changed his Life** | Jennifer Taylor |

## MEDICAL

| | |
|---|---|
| **An Inescapable Temptation** | Scarlet Wilson |
| **Revealing The Real Dr Robinson** | Dianne Drake |
| **The Rebel and Miss Jones** | Annie Claydon |
| **Swallowbrook's Wedding of the Year** | Abigail Gordon |

0113 GEN STD HB

# ROMANCE

|  |  |
|---|---|
| **Banished to the Harem** | Carol Marinelli |
| **Not Just the Greek's Wife** | Lucy Monroe |
| **A Delicious Deception** | Elizabeth Power |
| **Painted the Other Woman** | Julia James |
| **Taming the Brooding Cattleman** | Marion Lennox |
| **The Rancher's Unexpected Family** | Myrna Mackenzie |
| **Nanny for the Millionaire's Twins** | Susan Meier |
| **Truth-Or-Date.com** | Nina Harrington |
| **A Game of Vows** | Maisey Yates |
| **A Devil in Disguise** | Caitlin Crews |
| **Revelations of the Night Before** | Lynn Raye Harris |

# HISTORICAL

|  |  |
|---|---|
| **Two Wrongs Make a Marriage** | Christine Merrill |
| **How to Ruin a Reputation** | Bronwyn Scott |
| **When Marrying a Duke...** | Helen Dickson |
| **No Occupation for a Lady** | Gail Whitiker |
| **Tarnished Rose of the Court** | Amanda McCabe |

# MEDICAL

|  |  |
|---|---|
| **Sydney Harbour Hospital: Ava's Re-Awakening** | Carol Marinelli |
| **How To Mend A Broken Heart** | Amy Andrews |
| **Falling for Dr Fearless** | Lucy Clark |
| **The Nurse He Shouldn't Notice** | Susan Carlisle |
| **Every Boy's Dream Dad** | Sue MacKay |
| **Return of the Rebel Surgeon** | Connie Cox |

# Mills & Boon® Hardback

## March 2013

## ROMANCE

| | |
|---|---|
| **Playing the Dutiful Wife** | Carol Marinelli |
| **The Fallen Greek Bride** | Jane Porter |
| **A Scandal, a Secret, a Baby** | Sharon Kendrick |
| **The Notorious Gabriel Diaz** | Cathy Williams |
| **A Reputation For Revenge** | Jennie Lucas |
| **Captive in the Spotlight** | Annie West |
| **Taming the Last Acosta** | Susan Stephens |
| **Island of Secrets** | Robyn Donald |
| **The Taming of a Wild Child** | Kimberly Lang |
| **First Time For Everything** | Aimee Carson |
| **Guardian to the Heiress** | Margaret Way |
| **Little Cowgirl on His Doorstep** | Donna Alward |
| **Mission: Soldier to Daddy** | Soraya Lane |
| **Winning Back His Wife** | Melissa McClone |
| **The Guy To Be Seen With** | Fiona Harper |
| **Why Resist a Rebel?** | Leah Ashton |
| **Sydney Harbour Hospital: Evie's Bombshell** | Amy Andrews |
| **The Prince Who Charmed Her** | Fiona McArthur |

## MEDICAL

| | |
|---|---|
| **NYC Angels: Redeeming The Playboy** | Carol Marinelli |
| **NYC Angels: Heiress's Baby Scandal** | Janice Lynn |
| **St Piran's: The Wedding!** | Alison Roberts |
| **His Hidden American Beauty** | Connie Cox |

0213 GEN STD HB

# ROMANCE

| | |
|---|---|
| A Night of No Return | Sarah Morgan |
| A Tempestuous Temptation | Cathy Williams |
| Back in the Headlines | Sharon Kendrick |
| A Taste of the Untamed | Susan Stephens |
| The Count's Christmas Baby | Rebecca Winters |
| His Larkville Cinderella | Melissa McClone |
| The Nanny Who Saved Christmas | Michelle Douglas |
| Snowed in at the Ranch | Cara Colter |
| Exquisite Revenge | Abby Green |
| Beneath the Veil of Paradise | Kate Hewitt |
| Surrendering All But Her Heart | Melanie Milburne |

# HISTORICAL

| | |
|---|---|
| How to Sin Successfully | Bronwyn Scott |
| Hattie Wilkinson Meets Her Match | Michelle Styles |
| The Captain's Kidnapped Beauty | Mary Nichols |
| The Admiral's Penniless Bride | Carla Kelly |
| Return of the Border Warrior | Blythe Gifford |

# MEDICAL

| | |
|---|---|
| Her Motherhood Wish | Anne Fraser |
| A Bond Between Strangers | Scarlet Wilson |
| Once a Playboy... | Kate Hardy |
| Challenging the Nurse's Rules | Janice Lynn |
| The Sheikh and the Surrogate Mum | Meredith Webber |
| Tamed by her Brooding Boss | Joanna Neil |